THE THIRD LANE

Julie C. Round

OLDSTICK BOOKS

First Published in Great Britain in 2011 by
Oldstick Books
18 Wiston Close
Worthing
BN14 7PU

A CIP Catalogue of this book is available from
the British Library

ISBN 978-0-9557242-2-0

Cover Photos: ©istockphoto.com/

Portrait Photograph by David Sawyer
www.the-photographer.org.

Typeset in Garamond 12pt
by Chandler Book Design,
www.chandlerbookdesign.co.uk

Printed in Great Britain by the
MPG Books Group, Bodmin and King's Lynn.

To Ben
"for now is all the time..."
(Cindy Walker)

1

Katie hadn't meant to spy on her daughter.

At sixteen, Heather was very sensitive about her privacy and her possessions and her mother would never normally have looked in her school bag, but the English homework was on the dressing table and when she saw that it was a comparison between her family and one from a television programme she felt compelled to read on.

The family most like mine is the Harper family, but there are both similarities and differences. The characters in the programme are exaggerated for comic effect.

The father in the series is a dentist whereas my father is a conservationist, looking after trees and plants.

The mother has a job but seems to spend a lot of time making dreadful meals.

My mother is a good cook. She is a chiropractor and drives a silver estate car.

They are both bossy.

Their son is a sly nerd, but my brother Robert is easily led.

The Harpers have a lodger – a weird Welshman, while we used to have my Nan living with us, but now she has her own mobile home.

Katie was not a chiropractor – she was a chiropodist. Heather knew that – why wasn't she writing the truth?

It was also an exaggeration to call Bernard a

conservationist. It wasn't a lie – he thought like a conservationist, but his job was helping out in the garden centre.

Smallbridge Garden Centre had been built on the land that had been occupied by Katie's home, Lane's End. She and Rose, her mother, had sold the market garden when it became impossible to make it pay.

They had moved into a new house just the other side of Stable Lane and Rose had kept the camping site going for a few years but eventually that, too, was making a loss and she had to sell up.

To Katie's surprise her mother had then declared that she'd always wanted to travel round England and was about to do so before she was too old to drive safely.

Next thing they knew, Rose was preparing her home on wheels for the journey, explaining that, as Pat,her sister-in-law had recently lost her husband she now had someone who could accompany her.

Katie read on. She was surprised that Heather said little about her brother although she knew her daughter had gone through a difficult time when Robert started at the same school.

As he was a slow learner, the other children called him, "Rob the Rem." and Heather had suddenly found herself vulnerable to the teasing of her peers. They had found that mocking her brother had been an effective way of taking her down a peg or two.

Katie had noticed that Heather's response was to work even harder to prove how different she was from Robert and although this was creditable it had meant she had neither the time nor the inclination to help him when he was uncertain of his surroundings.

However, Robert had such a sunny disposition and was so eager to please and willing to try that pupils and teachers alike warmed to him.

He soon had a gang of friends who liked and supported him.

He became, "Robbie," and the name stuck, so that the "Bob," from earlier years was dropped, even at home.

It was a stark little piece of writing – not up to her usual standard, thought Katie. It was as if Heather wanted to keep her real family secret.

Perhaps she was going to add some more – write about how the members of each family interacted, making it more personal, more interesting.

Katie tried to imagine what she would write – how she would describe their family.

Bernard would come first, of course, her husband, the man who had grown from a simple, lonely, troubled individual to a confident worker and loving father.

Bernard – or, as she affectionately called him, Ned, still had problems reading and writing, but starting afresh with his son, and learning at his pace, had gained extra confidence so that they could now enjoy reading comics together.

She loved hearing them as they took parts – Robert reading the small print and his father adding the passages in capital letters.

There had been a time when they thought Robert would never learn to read but gradually they had found that each complemented the other.

They were helped by computer programs that

Bernard's friend Zak sent them, their favourite being a man who climbed a ladder to collect letters and make them into words. Bernard had always had difficulty with small letters but was forced to learn them for his son's sake.

Robbie was ten years old before he could read simple sentences but it didn't seem to bother him. He had one abiding passion. He loved animals, and they seemed to respond to him.

All Katie's efforts to keep the garden pet free had evaporated as her son brought home stray creatures. True, they no longer had chickens, but they did have two cats, a hutch full of rabbits, a couple of guinea pigs, a pond with frogs and an aquarium with stick insects which lived in Robbie's bedroom.

Their old dog, Sandy, was arthritic and almost blind and spent most of the day indoors or in the garden and she feared would not be with them much longer.

That was one reason why they had not had a holiday away for years. It was Robbie's menagerie.

It hadn't seemed fair to ask Rose to take care of everything, as well as the campsite, but now it had all been sold they needed to arrange something before her mother headed off and they were stuck.

"What are you doing?"

Katie turned to face her challenger.

"I was just looking for washing," she replied. "I saw your homework on the desk. It's a good start."

"It's nothing to do with you. You're not my teacher. I'll decide when you can see my work."

"OK,OK. Don't get stroppy with me, young lady. I'm just interested, that's all."

"I don't want you checking up on me. I want a lock on my door."

"That's never been necessary before." Katie hated to feel that she was being shut out of her daughter's life.

"Well, it is now. I'll put my washing in the basket in the bathroom. I can change the sheets. There's no need for you to come into my room."

"Well try it without for a month and then, if you don't trust me, we'll ask Dad for a lock – but we'll have to have a spare key."

"At least that will keep Robbie out."

"He doesn't go in your room."

"He might. There's no knowing what his stupid friends might dare him to do."

"Heather!" Katie tried to laugh it off but it was true. Although Heather rarely brought friends home Robbie seemed to be extremely popular with both girls and boys.

Of course, Rose and Bernard had encouraged them. Rose had taken a group of them to the Wildfowl Centre and Bernard played football and cricket with them on the field behind the house.

Katie left her daughter to her studies. She's very driven, she thought, as if passing examinations was the most important thing in life. Still, it was preferable to spending all her time dreaming about boys or how to be famous, like other girls her age.

*

"I couldn't drive this!" exclaimed Pat, looking at Rose's home as a vehicle for the first time. "I thought you were going to park it here for ever."

"I can't, Pat. I have permission to carry on using the space until the garden centre expands onto the camping site – and then I'll have to move. Anyway, I bought a home on wheels so that I could travel in it."

6

"Have you driven it yet?"

"Not much. Enough to know that it's not much different from the van."

"It's so big, Rose."

"Not inside. I'm not sure we could both live in it for weeks at a time."

Pat was looking round intently as if she was planning how they would share the space. It wasn't unlike the houseboat that she and George had lived in when they left the pub, with lots of high lockers and folding furniture.

Rose knew they'd been sorry to leave the boat but George had begun to suffer bouts of dizziness and shortness of breath so it was too dangerous for them to stay.

"It's a good job I'm used to living in cramped quarters," Pat laughed.

"Do you think it's too cramped?" Rose looked worried.

"No, Rose. It's beautiful. Did they make it for you?"

"Yes. It was new. It still cost less than a flat like yours."

"Where did you plan to go?"

"Let's sit down and I'll show you. We'll have to wait until September but I wanted to get you used to the idea." She reached into a cupboard and pulled out a large map book. "I thought we might start by heading West and then go inland towards London, using the A roads, not the motorways. I've marked places where we can park not far from towns and villages. If we cross over into Kent and then come back along the coast it should be enough for the first trip. Is there anywhere you would like to see?"

"Canterbury. I've always wanted to visit the Cathedral."

"We could do that – but first we have to practice driving. I'll need you to know how in case there's an emergency."

"But I've only just got my licence. Don't we need a special one?"

"Not with this – it's what they call a Class B. I don't think they'd insure me for anything bigger at my age."

"Oh, Rose. It's so kind of you to think of this."

Not really, thought Rose. I've been waiting years for this opportunity.

"It's wonderful that you can come too," she said. "I'm so sorry about George but it'll be great having you with me."

Pat sighed. "It's all right, Rose. I didn't like to see him suffering. We had some good times, but it hasn't been easy since we left the pub."

"Well, let's start a new chapter. We'll use the early summer to practice locally, then take a break. I don't want to be on the roads during the school holidays.

I need to tell Katie and Bernard what we've planned. I think they are going up north in August."

"This is too much to take in, Rose. I'm not sure I'm brave enough."

"Of course you are. Go home and think about it."

Rose locked the door of the motorhome and waited until Pat had driven away – then slowly crossed the road to The Meadows.

It was such a long time since she'd done anything other than fit in with her daughter's plans – but now, at last, she was going to do something she wanted, before she was too old and set in her ways.

Heather was in her room, flat on her stomach on her bed, looking at a magazine.

Why couldn't she have tight shorts like those, and

ruched boob-tubes? It didn't mean she was offering anything – just that she wanted to look as attractive as the other girls. As soon as her exams were over she was going to try to get a job. She wasn't confined to the village. She had her bike. She could easily get into town.

She was supposed to save some of her allowance for holidays but she was fed up with holidaying with her parents. She needed some freedom.

She thought about the trip that was arranged for August. It would be nice seeing Ryan again. He was eighteen now and they hadn't been together for five years. Perhaps he'd feel she was too young for him. He might even be dreading their visit. Last time they met he'd been very much a boy's boy – only interested in football and fast cars. She'd felt they had very little in common and became unusually shy in his presence.

Now she wanted to show him how grown-up she was. She wanted to look fashionable, desirable even. Most of all she wanted him to notice her. She wanted to have an effect.

She'd forgotten what he was studying. Her mother had told her but she couldn't remember. Did he ever ask about her? she wondered. She would have to be careful not to boast about her expected grades. Did he know she wanted to go to University? She doubted it.

Perhaps there was something they could both compete in. She was sure she could outrun him but he probably had more strength. She wondered if he went surfing or ice-skating. She had prizes for swimming but preferred athletics.

The idea of competing against her childhood friend, and beating him, made her smile. If this was the last time she went on holiday with her parents she was going to make sure she enjoyed it.

She heard someone downstairs and went to the doorway to see who it was.

"Hallo, Nana. There's no-one in but me."

"That's all right. Would you like a cup of tea?"

"Thanks, Nan, I'd love one. How's Auntie Pat?"

"Bearing up very well. I'm going to take her on holiday."

"When?"

"In the autumn. We're going to take the motorhome. I thought it was time I did a bit of exploring."

Heather came down the stairs and followed her grandmother into the kitchen.

"That sounds mysterious. I wish I could come too."

"There's not enough room. Perhaps another time – but you have college to prepare for."

The back gate clicked and Sandy waddled towards the door to greet Robbie and his father.

They sat round the kitchen table and Heather watched as her brother fed the dog biscuit under the table.

"Will you take Sandy with you, Nana?" she asked.

"No, I'm afraid not. She's too old for a trip like that. Besides, Robbie can look after her as well as I could. She'll be happier here."

Heather felt the familiar stab of jealousy that praise of her younger sibling always evoked. Why was it that however hard she tried, however successful she was – it was always Robbie that brought a smile to people's faces?

To her he was a failure, someone with neither physical nor mental skills. He could hardly catch a ball, his reading was years behind his peers, he wasn't musical or artistic – yet something made people want to be with him. Angry people seemed calmer in his presence, hurt people were soothed, and the effect on animals was even more pronounced. Each different creature seemed to behave as if he were one of them.

"I'm going out," she said, rising from the table. "I'll be back for tea. I've got my phone." She'd go and look round the garden centre.

At first she hadn't understood why they called it Smallbridge Garden Centre when it was in Stable Lane – but then she realised most people had to drive into Smallbridge Lane to reach the car park, and it was certainly a more romantic sounding title. All the advertising had a picture of a small bridge over a river, not unlike where she had played Pooh-sticks with her father and his friend Zak when she was younger.

She'd look in the aromatherapy section and perhaps browse through the jewellery area. She'd not stay long. Although she liked looking round the place she felt embarrassed when she saw her father working there. If it hadn't been for that she might have tried for a summer job.

It had been a while since Rose had been with them for dinner. Katie was intensely aware of the division round the table.

Bernard and Robbie sat at one side, with Rose and Heather opposite, while she served from one end.

Robbie was trying to put everything on a slice of bread, as usual.

"Robbie. You can't have sandwiches all the time."

"Mum, sausage sandwiches are the best."

Bernard and Rose watched him indulgently but Katie caught the hint of a sneer on her daughter's face.

"Where were you off to this afternoon, then, Heather?" she asked lightly.

"Just the garden centre. The girls there don't seem too happy. I wanted to check on something but they couldn't help." She turned to her grandmother. "Nan, is there a box of jewellery around somewhere?"

"You mean Bernard's mother's. Yes, but it is probably in the loft. Do you know, Bernard?"

Katie watched her husband shrink into his seat. She knew he hadn't looked at anything belonging to his family for years. He'd probably forgotten what was in the box. She could remember seeing some papers, and a mountain of jewellery that his mother had collected. Now he looked uncomfortable.

Not being present when his mother had been killed in a road accident had made him feel guilty and miserable and Katie had encouraged him to put his past behind him and live only for the family he had around him.

"Yogurt and banana for pudding," she chirped, pushing back her chair in an effort to change the subject.

After the meal she tried to get Heather to help with the washing up. She wanted to stop her before she began to question Bernard about his youth.

Gradually, over the years Heather had wheedled out of her father details of his difficulties at school, constantly comparing her progress with his lack of ability until, "What WERE you good at, Dad?" became a question Katie was tired of hearing.

He's used to it, Katie thought. He's used to people underestimating him – but I'm not – and it shouldn't happen with his own daughter. Can't she see how important he is to us all? Can't she see how much he has achieved?

But, of course, she couldn't. Heather hadn't been born when Katie first met Ned, the artist, as he was then, a lost soul who'd been rescued by Eliza and trained to do mosaics.

Together the two women had watched him grow in confidence and then, when she had married him, had come the transformation into a competent gardener and the final partnership with her mother.

Heather had loved her father then and spent as much time with him as she could, but everything changed once Robert was born.

Katie had tried to make her feel appreciated. She'd tried to make up for the fact that Ned seemed to take more interest in the baby than his daughter – but she could sense they were drawing apart.

The more Heather succeeded, the more her father avoided her. It was almost as if she made him feel inadequate. Instead of being proud of her achievements he seemed to ignore them. It became Katie and her mother's task to praise and encourage the girl – but they could never quite match the closeness she and her father had shared before she started school.

Was this why Heather had tried to make out their jobs were more important than they really were? Was she trying to get people to admire her the way her father seemed incapable of doing?

Was there any harm in exaggerating, just a little bit? After all, she could understand her daughter not wanting to admit that her mother looked after people's feet for a living. She smiled. She could almost imagine herself doing the same thing. It was only a school essay –it wasn't an application or anything official.

She wouldn't mention it again.

2

Bernard was content. He liked the variety and colour of the garden centre. He liked the way the displays changed with the seasons, red poinsettias at Christmas, orchids and chrysanthemums, then the geraniums, his favourites. He loved the way their colours seemed to glow in the light, orange, cream, scarlet and pink. Roses might have the best scent but he wished they didn't have thorns.

He also liked the work.

At first the management only allowed him to pack and unpack, clean and lift, but when they saw the way he answered customers' queries and overheard his knowledgeable answers they began to look on him as a gardening advisor.

The manager realised Bernard had areas of expertise that complemented his own and would often direct the young part-time assistants to him for advice and training.

Although he didn't have an official title he had become a respected member of staff and was paid accordingly.

He looked up as he heard the back gate rattle. No-one should be delivering anything at this time of night. He went over and opened it a crack.

At first he didn't recognise the face that was staring at him. The boy was covered in mud. His hair was clumped with soil and there were tear stains down his cheeks.

As he raised his hands to rub his eyes Bernard could see they were scratched and bleeding.

Robert staggered forward and almost toppled onto him.

"Robbie! What happened?" asked Bernard, leading him to a bench and sitting him down.

Robbie let out a deep breath. "Boys," he stuttered, "some boys."

"What boys? What did they do?"

"The b-bastards pushed me down a hole."

"Why? What hole?"

"Badgers. I was looking for badgers." His breathing was more natural now and Bernard held his arms to stop him rubbing his eyes.

"Did you know these boys?" asked Bernard.

"No." Robbie was holding back tears.

"Some strange boys pushed you down a badger hole?"

Robert nodded. "I kicked," he ventured, "but I couldn't shout."

Bernard looked at his son's blackened face. His teeth were covered in mud and his face was striped with tears.

"Come on," he said. "Let's get you cleaned up."

Looking round to see if there were any customers about, Bernard held his son firmly and led him to the washrooms. A startled assistant brushed past them, but Bernard frowned and he made no remark.

He filled a bowl with warm water and, using paper towels from the dispenser, tried to gently wash the earth away from his son's eyes.

He had to keep using fresh sheets as they soon crumbled away as they became wet.

Once he had cleaned Robbie's face and brushed him down, Bernard swept the room, while Robbie, still shivering, soaped his hands in fresh hot water.

Trying to find out more about the incident Bernard

asked, "Did you talk to these boys?"

"They wanted to know what I was doing," said Robbie.

"And you told them you were looking for badgers?"

Robbie nodded. "Then one said I wasn't looking hard enough and they jumped on me. They shoved and shoved and I couldn't shout or my mouth would get full of dirt. They ran off and left me there." He tried to rub his hair with a paper towel but his hands were shaking.

Bernard leaned forward and put his arms round his son. Robbie was beginning to cry again and Bernard wanted to get him home in the warm as quickly as possible.

"You wait here," he said. "I'll just tell them I'm off and I'll let you out the side way." He wasn't known for his anger but he was feeling choked with rage.

Why should this happen to the kindest of boys? What could he do about it? He needed to talk to Katie.

Katie was glad to get home. The elderly lady whose feet she'd been tending had been particularly full of complaints about the other residents of her care home. Katie knew part of her job was to make her customers feel less lonely and more comfortable but sometimes it was almost impossible.

She had remained smiling and patient until she was back in the car but she wished that, just once, someone would pamper her to make her feel better.

The house seemed empty. Even Sandy the dog didn't get out of her bed under the kitchen table to greet her.

There was the sound of a key in the front door and she could hear someone running up the stairs.

Bernard came into the kitchen.

"Is that Robbie with you?" she asked.

"Yes – but he's not feeling too well."

Katie rose to her feet. "What's up? Has he been sick?"

"No. Sit down. He just needs to get changed."

"He's fallen into something… is he hurt?"

"No. He's fine – just a bit shook up. Some boys pushed him over."

"What boys? Where?"

"Boys he didn't know. He was in the woods. Don't fuss."

"I must see him." She leapt up and ran up the stairs. "Robbie! Where are you?"

"In the bathroom. I'm having a shower. Sorry about my clothes."

She glanced into his bedroom. There on the floor were his jeans and sweatshirt – covered in thick mud. She looked for signs of blood but saw none. Thank goodness for that, she thought and felt her racing heart slow down a little.

"Are you really OK, Son?" she called through the bathroom door. "Can I come in?"

"I'm fine, Mum. I'm coming out."

There was the sound of teeth being cleaned and water running away and Robbie emerged, his black curls flopping across his eyes and his face looking scrubbed and glowing. He was holding his towelling robe round him but he looked unscathed. She sighed with relief.

"Did someone hit you?" she asked as she followed him into his room.

"No. They just put my head down a hole. I'm all right, really. What's for dinner?"

She laughed, then, and, picking up the dirty clothing turned to go down the stairs.

"Your father gave me a fright," she said. "How about a cup of tea?"

After dinner, when Heather was reading on her bed, there was a knock on her bedroom door.

"Who is it?" she called.

"Me. Robbie. Can I come in?"

"What do you want?"

Robbie pushed the door open and stood waiting. "I want my hair cut," he said.

Heather looked at her brother. She had often envied his dark shiny curls. They swept round his ears in a most unfashionable style but made him look romantic and attractive. Her own hair was plain in comparison, just long and a shade of honey blonde that was neither golden nor brown.

"Why come to me?" she said.

"I didn't want to ask Mum," he admitted. "She might not like it."

"Why? What sort of haircut do you want?" She found herself warming to the idea.

Robbie stepped into the room and closed the door behind him.

"I want a soldier's cut," he explained, "Short."

"You want a number one?"

Robert looked blank, so she looked round the room for a magazine. Had she got a picture of someone with really short hair? She began to feel a tingle of excitement. This was something she would enjoy doing to her brother. She knew her mother would be furious – but if she was only doing what he'd asked – what would be the harm?

She leafed through the pages while Robbie stood

looking over her shoulder. At last she found a picture of a man with close cropped hair.

"There. Is that what you want to look like?" she asked.

Robbie hesitated. She guessed he'd imagined something slightly longer, more American.

He picked up the book and studied the photograph.

"Yes," he said at last.

"You could go to a barber's," she said.

"No. I want you to do it."

"Right. When?"

"Now?"

"No. I can't do it without clippers and we need to be sure we won't be interrupted. I'll tell you when. Let me think about it."

She dismissed him with a wave. She'd trimmed hair before – girls were always trying new styles – but this would be a radical change. She needed to buy or borrow some clippers and she could do with watching someone who knew what they were doing before she embarked on the task. Robbie would just have to wait.

Two days later the pair of them were in Heather's room, Robbie with a towel round his neck, staring at himself in the mirror.

Heather had been given a key for her door but had never used it. Now she felt uncomfortable as she turned it in the lock. It felt as if it was a signal that she was doing something she should not.

At first she snipped off his quiff and then moved round his head trimming the long strands with scissors. Once she was satisfied that she could see the shape of his head she took a deep breath and ran the clippers across his scalp.

"Keep still," she ordered as Robbie moved to get a

better view of what she was doing. She felt afraid and exhilarated, like the feeling she had when riding a roller coaster. She couldn't stop now. She had to continue. As she grew bolder it felt smoother and easier, until she looked with dismay at the back and had to decide whether to shave next to the skin or try to cut a straight line.

"It won't go straight," she told Robbie. "I'm going to have to follow your hair line."

"It doesn't matter," replied her brother. "Just do it." He rubbed the stubble on his head. "It feels odd," he grumbled.

"It was what you asked for," snapped Heather. "It's the best I can do." She gathered the loose hair up in the towel. "You'd better get in the shower and wash it properly. Is that what you wanted?"

The two of them stared at the face in the mirror. The soft, gentle looking boy had gone – replaced by a severe, rather startled young man – until Robbie smiled and then he looked as handsome as ever.

Heather was proud of her efforts. She'd tried to spoil her brother's looks but instead had made him look older, less vulnerable. She could see now why he had asked for the haircut and was surprised at his perception.

"I'll just get rid of this," she giggled. She'd never imagined she could feel this way about her brother. Fancy, just cutting his hair had brought them closer together.

Robbie grinned. "Thanks, Heather," he said.

It was their grandmother who was the first to see the new Robbie.

She'd been told about the incident in the woods but, short of saying he should never go anywhere alone, there was nothing the adults could think of to prevent it happening again.

Sandy was too old to be much protection but Robbie had been taking her with him when he was not going too far.

He brought Sandy with him when he visited Rose but, for once, it was not the dog that attracted his grandmother's attention.

She gave a gasp of surprise and then stood away from him to get a better view.

"When did you get that done?" she asked at last.

"Heather did it. Do you like it?"

"It's certainly different. Yes. I think I do. What does your mother say?"

"She hasn't seen it yet. Will you come with me?"

Rose laughed. "Sure. We'll face her together."

They needn't have worried. After the initial shock Katie and Bernard seemed to accept it. Katie did say, "It will soon grow back," and insist that, from now on, he used a proper barber.

They were surprisingly easy on Heather, too and Rose went home content that her family were, at last, beginning to understand each other.

Next morning Rose sat next to Pat as she turned out of Stable Lane and towards the bridge. She had manoeuvred the motorhome out of the car park and taken her sister-in-law through the controls.

"It's very high up," was Pat's only comment.

She went very slowly over the little bridge and then seemed to relax as she realised the road was quiet and there was very little traffic coming from the opposite direction.

By the time they reached the White Hart Rose felt she had done enough. "Pull into the car park, Pat. We'll have a cool drink and then I'll drive us back through the village."

"Thanks, Rose. I'm not used to concentrating so hard," said a relieved Pat. "Just wait until I tell Ed what I've just done."

"You should come over more often," said the landlord. "Tuesday is darts night, Pat. You always liked that."

"George was the expert," said Pat, "But I would like to come sometime." And she told them about the proposed trip.

"You're going together in the motorhome?" asked Ed.

"Yes," answered Rose, "The garden centre is going to start building on the campsite soon and I'll need to move on."

"You're welcome to park in the field behind the pub," he said. "It's a bit near the river but it would do as a temporary measure."

"That's very kind, Ed. The sooner I shift the better."

"Don't thank me. I've got an ulterior motive. How about helping behind the bar, Pat - just summer lunchtimes?"

"I'd love to, Ed. I've really missed it."

Rose watched as Pat's face lit up. If only she could find something that made her feel like that. Now they could no longer use the camping field there was nothing left for her to do. She was beginning to feel old and useless.

She would be counting the weeks until she could get away.

Heather did find work, as a waitress in a coffee shop in town. After two days she was regretting it. She felt awkward and clumsy. She hated being rushed and felt totally exhausted and miserable when she got in the way, or forgot instructions.

Every night she collapsed into bed after a hot bath, glad that she would have a break after four weeks, but dreading going back for the Bank Holiday.

"I can't hack it, Mum," she said, the Friday before they were going away. "I've told them I'm not going back. It's ruining my feet."

She was right. The little competitive running she had done during the summer had seen her times increase, but not as much as her rivals.

"I was going to suggest you switch to hurdles," her coach had said, "But until your form improves it wouldn't be any good."

"It's my summer job," said Heather. "I didn't realise how hard it would be. When we come back from Durham I'd like to try out."

"Well, have a good rest. I think you need it."

The holiday was only a week. Heather wanted to be back for her exam results.

It was hot and stuffy in the train. Heather sat listening to music and Robbie stared out of the window. Katie tried to read a magazine but didn't seem able to relax. Bernard was fidgeting next to her, seemingly unable to get comfortable with his legs under the table.

"Oh, go for a walk," she said at last. "Perhaps when you come back you'll be able to go to sleep."

But sleep was impossible with a carriage full of families with children, many of them munching on picnics or using play stations.

Robbie had a large activity book with dot-to-dot

pictures and puzzles. When his father returned they took turns tracing the mazes and finding the solutions to the 'Find the difference' pictures.

Heather put down her iPod. Bored, she turned to her mother. "Have you got a drink, Mum?" she asked.

"Yes, but leave some to go with your sandwiches."

"Is it lunch time?" asked Bernard.

"I suppose it could be. The picnic is under the table."

They were eating their sandwiches when Heather suddenly said, "I was thinking of going vegetarian."

"What made you decide that?" asked Katie.

"You had a stage when you wouldn't eat chicken!" Heather said, defensively. "Well I think it would be healthier and better for the planet if we didn't eat meat."

"Well, wait until you get back from holiday," said Katie calmly, determined not to be aggravated by her daughter. "It's not so easy when you're eating out."

By the time they reached their destination the family could hardly wait to get out of the train. They had a short walk to their lodgings. Katie's friend Lisa's house was too small for them to stay, but she'd found them a comfortable bed and breakfast nearby and had invited them for a late supper.

Heather scrabbled for her case and headed for the bathroom. "I need to change, stupid!" she said when her brother asked why she was in such a rush.

Katie knew what was on her daughter's mind but said nothing. It would be time enough when they got to Lisa and John's for her daughter to find out where Ryan was.

3

"Wine or beer, Bernard?" asked John when they'd all got settled in Lisa's lounge.

"Could I have a shandy, please, John?" was the reply.

"I'd like wine," said Katie, "And the kids will have lemonade, please."

Heather made a face at Robbie but he didn't seem to notice. He was staring at the long table at the other end of the room. It was laid ready for a meal and she realised her brother must be hungry.

"It's a casserole," said Lisa, "I hope that's OK."

Heather shrugged at her mother's warning frown. She would eat whatever she was given. She was tired, but not too tired to count the number of place settings.

"Is Ryan not here?" she asked.

"No, Heather. He's camping with the Territorials. He's applied to join the army. They're away for a long weekend. He'll be back on Tuesday."

Tuesday! How could she wait until Tuesday?

They did manage to fill in the time.

The next day the family went ten pin bowling. At first they played girls against boys but her father was so good and her mother so poor that they soon changed to adults versus children. Even then the grown ups won. Robbie's coordination was weak and Heather lost interest when she realised they couldn't win.

Monday saw them at the coast – eating fish and chips in a quayside restaurant. Katie tried hard to get everyone interested in historic ships but the weather was damp and they were all glad to get back to their lodgings.

Deprived of her lap-top Heather sat on her bed and texted her friend Shona.

Going mad wondering what Ryan will think of me. M and D have asked his family out for a pizza on Wed. Don't know what to wear. My hair's a mess. H.

She soon had a reply from Shona.

Good luck. Bet you look gorgeous. See you. S.

Some holiday this was turning out to be, nothing like the trips to Italy or Florida that her fellow students had boasted about.

What had her mother said they were doing tomorrow? Walking along the river bank, visiting the Cathedral and shopping. At least the shopping might be interesting, if they had any decent shops up there.

Wednesday evening arrived at last and Heather looked nervously at her reflection.

She'd tried putting her hair up but decided against it and her newly washed locks tumbled over her tight black top. She wore hooped white earrings and a short white skirt. Her legs were bare and her golden strapped sandals showed off her lilac painted toenails. She had four white and lilac bangles on one wrist and a new white bag. She didn't dare put perfume behind her ears. Her mother would know she was trying hard to impress. She was as ready as she would ever be to see Ryan again.

"Hi, Heather," Ryan smiled as they lined up in the doorway of the restaurant. It was very busy and they had to wait for a table.

Heather felt herself blush. Her heart was beating so loudly she was certain he could hear it. He was still the same height as her, but stocky, muscular even, with his strong square face and his brown eyes seeming to laugh at her.

"Hi, Ryan." Why hadn't she prepared something clever to say?

"How's things?" he said carelessly.

"Good. I hear you're joining the army."

"Yes, the Signals. I go next month. I can't wait." He turned away and gave Robert a friendly punch on the arm. "D'you like it here, big boy?"

Robert chuckled with delight. "Yes, Ryan. Dad said we could go to a deer park tomorrow."

The conversation was cut short as they were directed to a large table and Heather was thrilled when Ryan sat down next to her.

"What do you want, Heather?" asked her mother.

"A vegetable one, please," said Heather.

"Meat feast for me, please, Mrs Longman," said Ryan.

Heather tuned out the other choices while she studied his profile. What could she do to make him take more notice of her?

"What do you all do in the evenings round here?" she asked.

"Plenty. There's the ice rink and the college students put on plays. I'm going to one tomorrow night. My girlfriend's in it."

Heather felt as if she had swallowed a brick. Her fists clenched under the table. A girlfriend! That was a shock.

She'd waited until the holiday was nearly over to impress him and now he told her he had a girlfriend.

She bowed her head over her pizza. Of course, he was eighteen. It was to be expected. Yet somehow she'd always hoped that when they grew up they would be together. The holiday was completely ruined. Whatever they did now – all she wanted was to get back home and find out her exam results.

She'd got college to look forward to. There would be boys there who would probably be far more intelligent than a mere soldier.

She picked at the salad on the side of her plate. It was difficult to swallow.

Her mother and Lisa were chatting away. John and her father were eating silently and Ryan seemed to have turned his attention to Robbie.

As usual, she was the one left out – but she'd show them. "Can we go ice skating, Dad?" she called out, "On Friday – before we go home?"

"Ask your mother," replied Bernard, "I'm not sure some of us would be very good at it."

He's thinking of Robbie, thought Heather, but she was determined to show she could excel at something before they left.

"I'll take you," said Lisa, to Heather's surprise. "It's a while since I've been. We could go early in the morning before it gets too crowded."

"Thanks, Lisa," said Katie. "She doesn't like being penned up with us."

Heather scowled. Her mother was making her seem like a truculent teenager.

Still, if she could impress Lisa she'd feel the holiday hadn't been a complete waste of time.

"You want an ice-cream, Heather?" her mother was asking.

"No thanks, Mum. I've had enough." Wasn't that the truth!

"Don't you look the part!" exclaimed Lisa when Heather arrived on Friday morning.

"They're new leggings," grinned Heather, feeling more relaxed than she had for days.

"I'll just be a tick. Ryan's taking us in his car."

Heather stiffened. That wasn't what she'd expected. What if he was really good and made her look like a novice? She couldn't bear to be embarrassed by him.

"Does he skate?" she asked.

"Just a bit." He'd come up silently behind her and his deep voice made her jump.

"But I'm not very good. I expect you're brilliant."

"I'm not good at all." She began to warm to his ready smile. "I've only had a few sessions. We haven't got a permanent site near us."

"We should be well matched, then, as usual," he teased, and she felt the old feeling of companionship returning.

He even held her elbow as she climbed into his car and she hugged the feeling to herself as the three of them drove off to the ice rink.

It was the best morning Heather had had all week.

Lisa was a revelation. She was a skilful ice skater and left the two youngsters together to find their feet.

It didn't take Heather long to control her balance and,

as neither of them seemed to want to skate alone, they skated as a pair, daring each other to try out new moves and picking each other up when they fell. Gradually they gained in confidence until they ended up breathless and laughing in each other's arms.

"Want a drink, you two?" came a voice behind them.

"Yes, please," answered Ryan. "I'm starving."

And I'm confused – thought Heather. Can't he feel how good we are together? Yet he treats me like a younger sister. How will I ever get him to see me as anything else?

Heather's exam results were even better than she'd dared hope.

She'd passed all her GCSE's. Although she had a C for Maths and French, she had A's for Chemistry, Biology and Physics and A stars for English and P.E.

"We're going to celebrate with a midnight feast on the beach," said her friend Shona. "Can you get away?"

"I'll try," replied Heather. "Where are you meeting?"

"By the beach café. Darren suggested the pier but we thought it would still be too busy so near the centre of town."

"I'll have to cycle. I wish I didn't live so far out."

"Well, bring what you can. It will be fun."

Heather wasn't so sure. Getting out wouldn't be a problem but getting back in could be tricky. If her mother caught her she'd go ballistic.

But wasn't it time she did something a bit daring? Didn't she deserve a bit of excitement?

She could almost feel imaginary wings sprouting from her shoulder blades. She felt compelled to tell someone how she felt.

There was only one person she could safely let into the secret - Chantelle, her grandfather's partner.

Chantelle and James lived in the Lake District and, in spite of the fact that her grandfather had forfeited all contact with his family when they ran away together; Heather had begun to e-mail her old friend as soon as she knew her address.

Although she was now in her early forties Heather had found her understanding and sympathetic and a much more satisfying contact than the people her peers networked with on chat lines.

Hi Chantelle, wrote Heather, *We are back from Durham. It was a disaster. Ryan was gorgeous but he not only has a girl friend but he's joining the army. It was so boring being with the family all the time. Next year I want to do something really different.*

My results were fine – although my Maths let me down. I'm going to do some sort of Science and PE at college – probably with Business Studies.

A few of us are having a beach party tonight. Did you ever do anything like that? I don't get down to the sea often enough and I've never been there at night. I daren't say I am going to Shona's or my mum will phone there and check up on me.

I suppose I could tell Robbie but he might split to Dad. I'll take my phone and tell you all about it when I get back. Love, H..

Satisfied, she closed the lid of her lap top just in time to hear a gentle knock on her door.

"Heather. We have a surprise for you. Can you come down?" Now how was she going to get prepared for the party?

Heather opened the door. "Yes, Mum. What is it?"

"We've booked a table at the Italian restaurant in town. We're taking you out to dinner to celebrate. How about that?"

Heather tried to look delighted. She felt the smile stiffen on her face.

"Wow. That is a surprise," was all she could say in response.

"We're proud of you, darling. Nan and Pat are coming too. We have to be there by seven," and her mother stepped forward to hug her.

Heather felt tears of frustration form in her eyes. She gave her mother a squeeze and turned away.

"I'd better find something to wear," she choked.

"And I'll get in the bath before the men folk need to clean up," laughed her mother.

"Dim, dim, dim," Heather snarled once the bedroom door was closed behind her.

How could they be so dim as to think another meal out with them would be her idea of a treat? If only her college was further away. She was going to have to live at home for at least the next two years – but after that… After that she would find a University that was as far away as possible. It wasn't just her Nan that wanted to travel. She wanted to get away – away from the country lanes to somewhere light, bright and exciting.

Meanwhile, she might still be able to join the beach party. It depended on how late it was when they returned from town. Hopefully they would be so tired that they would go to sleep quickly. She'd pack up some warm clothes and find some crisps and a torch – she'd like to take a flask but the others would call her a wimp. Would Robbie miss one of his cans of coke? She didn't really like the stuff but she would need a drink. It was a dry evening and if she wore jeans and trainers it wouldn't matter if the tide came in.

Her anger had vanished with her determination not to let the family's plans spoil her own. She was grateful they cared but wished with all her heart they were not quite so blind to her feelings and so desperately old fashioned.

The meal was not the success Katie had hoped for.

Heather was unusually silent and it was left to Pat to dominate the conversation.

She was telling Katie about her flat. "Here's the spare keys. That's the main door and that's the one for my door. The heating is off, but if it gets frosty I've left instructions in the kitchen drawer. I don't get much post. There's a box in the main hallway and if you could empty it once a week that should be sufficient."

"Calm down, Pat," said Rose. "You aren't going to be away long enough to worry."

"I'm not worried. I'm looking forward to it."

"It's all change for us," said Rose, turning to her granddaughter, "and aren't you excited about your new college?"

"It's only down the road, Nan. It's hardly an adventure."

"She's going to study Physics, PE and Business Studies," said Katie, proudly.

"My, that should keep you busy."

Heather just nodded. It wasn't Physics she was going to study – it was Sports Science, but she couldn't be bothered to correct her mother. She'd finished her meal and was fidgeting with her bag.

"Would you all like tiramisu?" asked Katie.

"Yes, please, Mum," replied Robbie. They all concurred, even Heather, although she did check her watch.

I wonder if she's arranged something for later? thought Katie. She probably wants to talk to her friends or chat on line. She's drawing away from us. I've got to let her grow up. I remember that feeling – when what is going on inside your head seems so much more important than what's happening around you.

"Right. A toast to our star student and then we'll have our pudding and coffee."

Bernard and Robbie raised their glasses. They'd both had coke, while the rest of them had shared a bottle of wine.

Katie felt Bernard's hand reach for her under the table. Perhaps he, too, had felt the gathering had shown up the differences between them all, rather than binding them together.

She had the horrible feeling that the next few years would see the family fragmenting and that she and her husband would be left on their own. What would she do then? She didn't want to think about it. She was too tired. It was time to go home.

4

Heather ran up the stairs to her room. It was about eleven o'clock. She had plenty of time to get changed and down to the beach. Waiting until everyone else was in bed would be the hardest part. She'd put on her nightclothes to go to the bathroom and then wait until the house was quiet. She didn't think the adults would stay up for long. They both had to work in the morning.

By half past eleven everyone had retired to their own rooms. Heather was in her jeans, a warm sweater and a waterproof parka. If she could get down the stairs without alerting Robbie she was sure she could escape detection.

No-one seemed to be disturbed as she collected the food and drink she had secreted in the kitchen. The dog blinked at her as she opened the back door but didn't appear to want to move.

"Good dog, Sandy. You stay there," whispered Heather and, closing the door gently behind her, went to get her bike from the shed.

She unlocked the door and pulled out her bicycle. The moon gave enough light for her to see to lock up again and wheel the bike through the back gate before turning on the headlight.

As she lifted herself into the saddle she realised how tense all her muscles had been. She looked back at the house. There were no lights in the windows. She gave a sigh of relief. She'd managed it! She was free to go to the party. She wanted to laugh out loud but instead felt her face split into a wide grin. This was better than any dinner party with 'the olds'. This was fun.

There was a tiny wood leading from the road to the beach and the partygoers had lit a fire at the seaward end so that it was hidden from the houses along the front by the trees. Someone was playing a guitar and a few people were clambering among the rocks with torches, hunting for crabs.

The sea was black and silver and making a pulsating swishing noise, unlike anything she had heard in the daytime. She realised she should have brought a blanket to sit on and looked around for someone she knew, hoping she could share.

Fiona and Jason were wrapped in each other's arms and she didn't want to sit on the cold rocks or the wet sand so she moved towards the fire.

"Hi, Heather," said Stephen – who was toasting sausages over the flames.

She gestured towards a box that was visible under the trees. "Will that take my weight?"

"Sure. Have a seat. You want something to eat?"

"Not yet. We had dinner late."

"Can you get some rolls out before you sit down?"

She lifted the lid and found the bread, passing him a bag of rolls. As their fingers touched she felt a new closeness. There was something about the way he was looking at her. His hair was long, too long she had always thought, and his eyes were dark and deep set. He wasn't her type at all – yet his hands were soft, with long, slender fingers. She'd never noticed them before and now, as she watched the broad smile creep across his face she knew that she had made a connection.

"Can I help you give out the food?" she asked, wanting nothing more than to stay near him.

"Yes – but you'll lose your seat. Everything we need is in that box."

She laughed. Even his voice sounded different. It warmed her just to listen to him.

"I don't suppose you've got drink as well?"

"Have a look – but don't tell everyone. The rum is just for special friends."

Once again her heart leapt at the tone of his voice. She wanted to feel him touch her again. "I'll take some round, shall I?" she asked.

"Just yell. They'll come if they want it."

She called out "Food's ready," and saw the guitarist put down his instrument. More people had arrived and people were dancing to a music player. A couple disappeared into the woods and Stephen turned to her,

"What about a drink?"

"I brought coke."

"That's perfect. Rum and coke. I've got some plastic cups. Let's try it."

He spread his coat on the ground in front of the box and opened the bottle. Half filling the cups he took the can of coke from her and topped up the drinks.

"Here, that'll warm you up."

Heather giggled. Sitting next to him with the whole of one side of her body tingling with his closeness, she was already warm.

At first they sat silently, watching the others, sipping their drinks. Then he seemed to remember that she was with him.

"You're going to be at the college, aren't you?" he said.

"Yes. I'm doing PE."

"I'm doing tennis, with the academy."

"I didn't know you were so sporty."

"What did you think I would take?"

"Oh – Art, Music – that sort of thing."

"I do like art. I like drawing people. I'd like to draw you."

"Oh, yeah – doing what?"

"Running. I take photographs and then draw from them. I'll show you one day."

"You are full of surprises." She looked at him archly and he responded in the way she'd hoped he would. He leaned over and kissed her, knocking her almost empty cup out of her hand as he pushed her backwards onto the box.

His kiss was disappointing. He tasted of salt and smoke and coca-cola. The position she was in was uncomfortable and she had to push him off to stop the box digging into her back.

"Let's dance," he said, taking a final swig of his drink and enveloping her in his arms as they rose together and began to sway to the music.

"Hey, Stevie. The fire's going out," shouted someone.

"Oh no, it's not," he whispered in Heather's ear – but she was no longer listening. Her head was beginning to ache and she felt sick.

She clung to him – hoping the pain would go away, but frightened that she might ruin the night by vomiting all over him.

"Steve, I don't feel too good," she managed to whisper at last.

"You want to sit down?"

"I think I'd better go down to the sea." She shrugged

him off and stumbled down the beach. Her feet sank into the soft sand and she fell to her knees and retched into the water.

She didn't rise in time and an icy wave crashed against her arms and face. Shivering, she pulled herself out of the foam and hobbled over the pebbles to the trees.

"I think I'd better get home," she said, between chattering teeth.

"Do you want me to come with you?"

"No, it's OK. I've got my bike, thanks, Steve. I'll see you at college."

She was soaked through, whether from the sea or from sweating she wasn't sure, but she needed to be in bed. What a fool she'd made of herself. Her head throbbed so much she could hardly stay upright. At least there were no cars on the roads and she got home without incident.

The bike went back into the shed and she dripped into the kitchen, squinting at the clock. It was almost 3a.m.

Leaving her shoes under the sink she tiptoed up to her room and undressed. She needed the toilet but took time to wrap herself in her nightclothes before she ventured into the corridor. She didn't flush the loo but she did turn her light on when she returned to her bedroom.

If only she'd thought to make a hot water bottle before she came up. She put on a clean pair of socks and crawled under the covers. She lay there, cursing herself for not helping herself to pain killers while she was in the bathroom. She no longer felt sick but her head still ached. She shut her eyes and tried to will herself to sleep.

Eventually the warmth of the bed soothed her and she succumbed.

Heather could hear people moving about when she woke up in the morning.

She sat up in bed and surveyed the pile of clothes she'd left on the floor. She could probably get away with putting the underwear in the laundry basket – but what to do with the rest?

If she hid the sweater, wore the coat and took her jeans to be cleaned she hoped no-one would suspect that she'd been out most of the night. The sooner she got out into the fresh air, the better. At least it was Saturday, the day she often went to the pool.

Once she was dressed, and with her damp and sandy jeans bundled into a plastic bag, she ventured downstairs for breakfast.

Her mother had already left to keep an appointment with a client but Robbie and her father were eating toast and drinking tea.

"I'll just have some cereal, thanks," she responded to her father's cheerful greeting.

"Dad's taking me to work," said Robbie. "He's going to ask if I can help out in the pet store."

"They'll probably have you cleaning out the fish tanks," jeered Heather.

"I don't mind. I like it there."

You're easily pleased, thought Heather, finishing her cornflakes. "I'm off down town. I'll see you tonight."

She ran upstairs for her parka and, slinging her bag across her shoulders, went out to the shed for her bike.

Once she had deposited her jeans at the cleaners she felt more relaxed.

The swimming pool was possibly her favourite place.

Half of it was divided into lanes for serious swimmers and the other half left for the general public.

She did her usual ten lengths of front crawl, turned over for the backstroke and was forging through the water for the lengths of breaststroke when she spotted a familiar figure in shorts and a T-shirt at the side of the pool.

Annoyed at the interruption to her regime, she stopped. "What are you doing here?"

"Looking for you," answered Stephen. "Can you get out and pose as if you were going to dive in?"

"We aren't supposed to dive. Why should I do that?"

"I want a photo." He gave an almost imperceptible nod towards the jacket he had draped across his arm.

"You've brought a camera in here!"

"Yes – but don't make a fuss. I'm not photographing children. I was on the beach and saw you getting off your bike. Be a sport – quick, while her back's turned."

Heather glanced up at the lifeguard. She had climbed down from her high stool and was walking towards some teenagers who had been jumping into the pool.

Heather pulled herself onto the side, struck a pose and then dived smoothly back into the water, swimming under the surface until she emerged half way down the pool.

"I'll meet you in the café in half an hour," said Stephen and smiled innocently at the lifeguard as he walked away.

Heather completed her programme in high spirits. It was almost as if she had a date – with her first real boyfriend.

"How did you get in?" she asked when, dry at last, with a hot chocolate drink in front of her, she sat opposite him in the café.

"I just told them I wanted to join and asked to look round."

"Haven't you been here before?"

"No. I don't swim."

"Never?"

"No. I don't like water. I don't want to talk about it. Are you ready for Monday?"

"I think so. I've got everything they suggested. What do you want to do eventually?"

"I'd like to run my own leisure centre. Mum thinks she has a tennis prodigy on her hands but she's mistaken."

"What does your Dad think?"

"He's not around. It's just Mum and me. She used to play tennis for the county but now she works in the bowls shop."

"What does she think of your art work?"

"Not much. She says I could never make a living at it. She's probably right."

"What are you going to do with the photos you took today?"

"Print off the best ones. Say! Have you got time to pose on the beach for me. I'd love some shots of you with the sea and the pier as background."

"Fully clothed, I hope?"

"Of course," he laughed. "But if I can get the wind blowing your hair out behind you that would be a bonus."

Heather felt like a model, posing on a breakwater with Stephen taking photos of her. He really did make her feel good. Maybe he wasn't the best looking guy in college but he was funny and kind and obviously liked being with her. That was enough for now.

5

"We're going to see Winston Churchill's house first," Rose had told Katie. "Then, when we've found somewhere to stay I'm taking Pat to see the World Garden and she's taking me to the big shopping centre. That's all we've planned so far."

Now, as the little family watched the motorhome disappear over the bridge they stopped waving and fell silent.

It was the first time, thought Katie, that she and Bernard had been entirely responsible for their children. She trusted that her husband knew most of what Robbie was thinking and could anticipate his behaviour – but Heather was a different matter.

How much freedom should a sixteen year old girl have nowadays?

Was she keeping secrets? Who did she contact on e-mail?

Was their relationship strong enough for her to act as her daughter's confidante or was there something missing between them – something ingrained so deep that neither of them were conscious of it – but which prevented them from having that loving friendship that she had with her own mother?

Perhaps it developed with time, she thought, this feeling of complete relaxation and belonging when you were together, but perhaps only some mothers and daughters can be like that, while others are forever rivals.

"I must go back to work, love." Bernard's voice broke into her thoughts. "I'll see you later."

"Yes. Come on you two. I've promised Heather I'd show her something and this would be a good time."

Heather followed her mother into the house. "What did you promise to show me?"

"Well, it wasn't so much a promise as an idea. I found the jewellery box your grandmother left. I thought we could look through it and see if there was anything you'd like."

"I'm not really into old fashioned jewellery, but OK."

Katie ran upstairs and brought down the box. At first all they could see were papers – a wedding certificate – Anne Janet Sands and James Ronald Longman, a death certificate for Arthur Bernard Sands from Eastleigh, Southampton and a photograph of a man with a moustache in some kind of uniform.

"He's not a soldier," said Heather.

"No. It's an old railway uniform. That's what they used to look like in those days. What a moustache! I think he must have been a station master."

Once the papers had been put to one side the hoard of jewellery was revealed. There was a crystal necklace, several strings of beads, a cameo brooch, another box with a string of pearls and a collection of brooches, earrings and rings.

"Nothing looks very valuable," said Heather.

"I can't tell. Those could be rubies and the earrings are the right colour for emeralds. She must have had pierced ears. There's a nice silver chain and crucifix."

"That's my favourite." Heather picked up a necklace of wooden beads. "It's the only thing I could wear now.

The rest looks too old fashioned."

"I thought there might be something special," said Katie. "Never mind. You take the necklace, darling. I'll put the rest away. I'm sure I've seen something gold somewhere. It must have been my mother's."

A week later a card came from Rose and Pat.

Katie looked at the picture. It was a mosaic floor.

"Mum's been to a Roman Villa," she told Bernard. "Look at this design."

Bernard looked at it longingly. "I haven't done anything like that for a long time," he murmured.

"I'll read it to everyone over dinner," said Katie, taking it back. "Then Robbie can mark it on his map."

The double page of an old road map book had been stuck on the inside of Robbie's bedroom door. Bernard and Robbie were using it to plot Rose's journey.

"Why don't you Google it?" Heather asked once they were all together.

"It won't be there all the time, then," her brother had responded.

"It isn't as if they were going round the world. I don't see the point."

"Sit down and I'll tell you what they said," ordered Katie, her voice sharper than she'd meant it to be. Did Heather set out to annoy her or was she just being too sensitive?

Dear family. Hope you like the card. It's like the work Bernard used to do, isn't it?

Pat dragged me off to the shops but I sat in a café while she raced round. A gentleman carried her bags back and we have been invited for a drink. Now I'll have to dress up! Off to Canterbury tomorrow. Weather and van fine. Love, Nan.

Katie laughed. "Pat's up to her old tricks, then. I hope they enjoy themselves. I must see to the dinner. Here, pass it round."

After the meal the children cleared the table and Bernard filled the dish washer.

Was there a way he could start doing mosaics again? He could try decorating the garage wall, just for practice – or should he do small designs, like plates, or tiles? Tiles might sell at the garden centre. Perhaps he could make some with Christmas designs – a tree, an angel or a star. That would be easy. All he needed was the little bricks. He hoped the shop that Eliza had used was still there. If he could remember the name he'd look them up in the phone book. Art Shops. He'd look them up and ask Rose to… Oh no – his mother-in-law wasn't around. He'd have to ask Katie to take him. Meanwhile he'd try drawing some pictures, just to see if they looked good enough.

Heather was trying to concentrate on Business Studies. It all seemed so theoretical. She didn't even know if she'd ever need it.

The only good thing about it was that Stephen was in her group. He'd told her it was his birthday the following week and she was trying to think what to get him.

"I'd like a party – but there's no room at home and Mum doesn't like strangers coming to the house. She says it's too small but really it's because it is such a mess."

Heather had a plan- but she wasn't sure she dared go through with it. It would depend on who Stephen wanted to invite. Of course, most of them would be his tennis friends – but there were some arty types she hadn't met.

"I think we'll end up all going for a curry," he sighed when they sat together at lunch time.

"Why don't we get takeaway?"

"And eat it under the pier?"

"No. I know somewhere we could eat it – but it would be borrowed for the evening and you'd have to guarantee that no-one would trash it."

"I don't mix with that sort."

"But there'd be drink – wouldn't there?"

"And a few would smoke – would your friend mind that?"

"No. She smokes. Just limit the numbers, say it's a gathering, a few of us getting together to chill. We should be able to get away without attracting hangers on."

"I'll make some punch – then they won't know what's in it and we can keep topping it up with lemonade. Where is this place? Can we get there without transport?"

"Yes. That's what's so great. It's in town. I'll take you there after college tomorrow and you can see for yourself."

"Have you got a key?"

"Not with me – but I can get it. It's at home. This will be a blast."

Katie had put the key to Pat's flat in the back of the cutlery drawer. Heather had thought it an odd choice – but her mother wanted it hidden from sight –so that made it easier to borrow. If it wasn't missed when she took it to show Stephen she'd take that as a sign that it was safe to borrow it for one night. She'd arrange an alibi with Emma, telling her mother she was sleeping at a friend's house overnight. Now all she had to do was find a suitable present for her boyfriend.

Stephen was, surprisingly, concerned about using Pat's flat.

"It's an old person's place!" he'd exclaimed when he first saw it.

"Of course. It's my Great-aunt's – but look at the size of the room."

"And look at all the ornaments. You'll have to put all those away – and stop people using the bedroom somehow. I'm not sure this is a good idea."

"Oh, Steve. Come on. You only hear about bad parties. There must be hundreds of good ones where people don't get smashed. We'll make sure everyone leaves by midnight so the neighbours don't complain. Have you thought who to invite?"

Each of the eight people they decided upon were told individually and warned not to announce it at college or on the internet.

Heather was curious to see how their sporty friends got on with the more arty types Stephen had invited.

Before they arrived she handed Stephen a small box.

She had found it immensely difficult to find the right gift for his birthday.

She hadn't wanted to seem too slushy, but she'd wanted to give him something different.

She watched his face anxiously as he opened the lid and then let out a sigh of relief as the delight and surprise lit up his face.

"Gee, Heather. I don't know what to say. This is the best present ever."

He took out the slim silver chain with the circular medallion. "I've never had a St. Christopher."

"I'm glad you like it." She accepted his hug. "Now, put it on."

"Not everyone knows it's my birthday," he said.

"That's what you think. Wait 'till they get here."

The evening started well enough. Stephen's friend, Jack, put himself in charge of the music and kept it low enough for people to be able to talk.

Soon the mantelpiece was decorated with cards and Stephen was the owner of a pile of new CD's and DVD's.

He took orders for curry and they all sat round the big rectangular table in Pat's living room to eat it.

Heather didn't know exactly what was in the punch and soon found people were opening cans and bottles in the kitchen. The plastic cups she'd bought were ignored and, while she cleared up the remains of the meal the music got louder and the conversations noisier.

Shona had brought her boyfriend Dan but was spending her time selecting CD's and seemed to have transferred her attention to Jack.

Heather felt sorry for Dan. He looked the perfect athlete – big, strong, and blonde with blue eyes and a square chin – but his interests were limited and his conversation was almost exclusively about rugby.

Jack, on the other hand, was almost too slim, with auburn coloured hair teased into spikes and long, delicate fingers. His brown eyes had lashes that made girls envious and he had the gift of being able to listen, and seem interested in what his companion had to say. Heather wasn't surprised that Shona found him attractive.

Dan had brought a six pack of beer and drank most of it himself. He grabbed hold of Shona and hugged her to him. "Let's dance," he growled.

"Your breath smells," she retorted, pulling away.

"Wha'dya expect? I've just had a curry." He stood in the centre of the room, undecided.

"Leave it, Dan," said Emma, putting her hand on his arm.

"I'm going for a slash," he said, shaking her off.

Heather looked for Stephen. He was deep in conversation with Sophie – the only other unattached girl at the party. Who else could keep an eye on Daniel?

"Roy, Can you check on Dan?" she asked Stephen's tennis partner.

There was no use asking the other two. They were in a passionate embrace on the sofa.

"Sure, Heather, but then I'm off. I've got practice in the morning."

Heather checked her watch. It was twelve fifteen. They'd done well to keep things civilised for this long. No-one had tried to gatecrash and only Dan seemed really drunk.

Where was Emma? Heather looked in the kitchen but there was no sign of her friend. Roy was dragging Dan down the corridor and trying to persuade him to leave.

There was one other place Emma could be- in the bathroom.

Sure enough her friend was kneeling by the toilet, wiping her mouth with paper.

"I've been sick," she said, unnecessarily. "I'll just have a wash and then I'll be out of here."

"I'm going to make coffee for anyone who wants it," replied Heather, but as she returned to the kitchen there was an almighty crash. The music stopped and the girls could hear shouting from the living room.

Heather ran back to see Jack's CD player in pieces on the floor, but, even worse, Pat's TV with a cracked screen lying next to it. Shona was crying, Roy was sitting on a struggling Daniel and Jack was holding a bloodstained tissue to his face.

"Come on, Dan. She's not worth it," said Roy.

"Slag," shouted Dan as he wrenched one arm free and pushed Roy to one side.

Shona shrank into a corner and Jack gripped Dan's flailing fist while Stephen threw himself at his legs, bringing them all down in a mass of grasping hands and rolling bodies. At last a bruised and subdued Dan was lifted to his feet and escorted outside.

"I'll take Shona home," shouted Sophie as the others departed, leaving Stephen, Jack, Emma and Heather to survey the damage.

"I'm sorry, Jack," said Stephen.

"It goes with the territory, Bro'. I just wasn't expecting it."

"We'll help you clear up," offered Emma.

"What am I going to do about the TV?" said Heather.

"I'll get another one," said Stephen. "Let's have a coffee. Thanks for all the pressies, guys."

"I told you they knew," laughed Heather.

Two hours later the flat looked almost as if they had not been there. The smell of curry still lingered; the rubbish bin was full of cans and bottles; there was a wine stain on the carpet and a burn hole on the arm of the sofa, but when they sat the TV on its table and tried it, nothing happened.

"There was a bit of a rattle when we picked it up," said Emma.

"I'm not sure I can get the same make," said Stephen, thoughtfully.

"Then get a better one," said Heather. "I'll help pay for it. It was my idea to be here."

"You're going to have to confess," said Emma.

"I intended to. Once we'd done it no-one could stop us."

There was a giggle from Emma and then everyone began laughing.

"I didn't mean that." Heather blushed.

Jack laughed. "It's OK Heather – don't get uptight. We know what you meant."

The trouble was, once the thought had entered her head she couldn't stop wondering. Would Stephen like her to take their friendship to the next stage? Was she ready? Was he the one she wanted to be her first lover?

She realised with stark clarity that he wasn't. He hadn't tried to come on to her in that way and she didn't think that he would – unless he was influenced by others. She needed to get Jack and Emma out of the way.

"You've been great, you two, but haven't you got homes to go to?"

"I thought…" stuttered Emma.

"You can doss down at my place, if you like," offered Jack. "I'm staying at my sister's and she doesn't mind what time I get in."

"Thanks, Jack. See you on Monday, guys. I hope we didn't ruin your birthday."

"No – it was good," replied Stephen, waving them off.

Heather waited for him in the kitchen. "He'll have to get some more CDs," she said.

"He's cool. Don't worry. I'm glad they've left us alone." He moved closer.

"Don't get ideas. You can have the sofa. Pat's bedroom is out of bounds."

"Heather!" But his complaint was half – hearted.

Perhaps he was as reluctant to go further as she was, she thought.

Next morning Heather rode home slowly and waited until she could talk to her mother alone.

"How was Stephen's party?" came the question she had been dreading.

"I've got to talk to you about that."

"He didn't force you to do anything you weren't ready for?"

"No, nothing like that. It was where we held the party."

"It wasn't at his house?"

"No. It was at Auntie Pat's."

"You let him have his party at Pat's!"

"Yes, I'm sorry. Don't shout. It was all right at first."

"Then what happened?"

"We knocked over Pat's TV."

"And broke it?"

"Yes – but we'll replace it."

Heather watched as the colour rose in her mother's cheeks. She seemed to be having difficulty saying anything. The words were spitting out of her mouth and her hands were clenching and unclenching with fury.

"Pat trusted me with that key. What does the place look like?"

She looks like she wants to hit me, thought Heather. "Everything else is OK. Stephen says he'll fix it, Mum. I'm sorry, I really am." She was shaking now, and near to tears.

"I'm going down to see for myself. I'll deal with you when I get back."

The door slammed and Heather was alone. How she wished she hadn't done it, but it was too late now. She would have to take the consequences.

6

Hi Chantelle,
    I'm in big trouble. I borrowed the key to Pat's flat and let my boyfriend have his Birthday party there. It was OK at first – we had curry and listened to music and talked – but one boy got jealous because his girl was paying attention to the DJ and he started a fight.

Pat's TV got broken and we've got to replace it. I had to tell Mum and she went berserk. She's chained up my bike and said I can't have it until half term.

Worse still, she's taking me to college in the car every day and coming to pick me up!

I feel such a dope. How could she humiliate me like that? I wish I could run away like you did.

I won't though – not while I have the chance to be really good at something. I've been practising jumping mini hurdles and I think I've mastered the stride pattern. I'm better than anyone else in the club already. Just wait until next season. I think I've found my best event.

Chat again soon, H.

Hi Heather,
    You have been having a torrid time, haven't you?
    Don't think running away solves everything. It doesn't. I had to tell Mum and Dad where I was and they've not forgiven me.

Pat might be glad of a new TV and you can always make out it was your idea to get your Mum to chauffeur you to college. Going there on the bike can't be too much fun in bad weather.

I'm so envious of you, being at college. I had to find out how to run a business the hard way. Mind you, it has helped since James started producing Greeting Cards. We now have a thriving mail-order business. I'll send you some samples of Christmas cards to see if you'd like to use them. We can't afford to give them away but if you know anyone who would like to buy them please let us know.

Must go now. Stay strong.

Chantelle.

Christmas! Heather hadn't begun to think of that yet. It was barely October and the end of term seemed so long away. There had been too many changes in the last few weeks. Perhaps she'd feel more settled when her Nan returned.

*

Rose and Pat reached the outskirts of Canterbury mid morning. It was an attractive site – with a bus stop nearby, and they were soon in the centre of town.

"Let's have a coffee and a toasted tea-cake and then look round the cathedral," said Pat.

Rose was content to comply. There was a feeling of History about the place – giving her a sense of permanence, making her feel part of something that had existed for generations.

She followed Pat into the cathedral and was immediately struck by its size. Pat joined a group that were being shown round by a guide but Rose found a quiet corner behind a pillar and sat down.

She wanted to breathe in the beauty of the place, but just having time to herself brought thoughts that she had suppressed rushing into her head.

It was almost a vision. She could see it so clearly – Lane's End – her home for over 60 years, the two miners' cottages knocked into one and the vegetable plot behind them. Why had she allowed them to be destroyed? They had been a piece of history, and if those who went before her had known what was happening they would never forgive her.

Tears came to her eyes and, for the second time since she'd moved out, she felt a deep seated pain that seemed to spread from her stomach to her head.

She loved her little motorhome, of course, but the house she was born into – where she'd lived with her husband and daughter – where Bernard had found them and carried on their family – that had been a special place, and she'd let them turn it into a garden centre.

"I'm sorry," she said to the ghosts of the past, and her fingers gripped the golden bracelet she wore for good luck. "I will find my past, I promise. I'll find somewhere I belong, before it's too late."

Pat returned with a guide book and postcards. "That was so interesting," she said, "and we have an invitation for dinner tonight."

"What have you been up to?" said Rose, turning her head away and replacing her handkerchief.

"Guess who I just met? Charles and Gregory. They were so impressed with our itinerary they decided to follow us and see the cathedral too."

"I do wish you hadn't said yes. What time are we supposed to meet them?"

"Seven – and if the buses don't run late we can always get a taxi back."

Rose looked at her sister-in-law's face, glowing with anticipation. She'd have to give in, but tomorrow they'd head south. She wanted to get back to the coast.

"I really don't know what to wear," Rose was complaining once they'd returned to the van.

"Put on your cream blouse, that's dressy, and the black pleated skirt. Liven it up with a bit of jewellery and you'll look fine."

"I'm too old for this sort of thing."

"You aren't too old to go out to dinner with friends – it's nothing special."

Some friends! thought Rose. They'd only just met the two people in question and would probably never see them again.

"Godfrey is nice enough, isn't he?"

"Well, yes. He's very polite. He told me he was a widower and said he worked in import and export."

"Did you tell him about Lane's End?"

"Not really. I was explaining about our trip in the motorhome."

"That's good. Now, what do you think of this?" Pat twirled round, resplendent in a burgundy trouser suit and dangling silver earrings.

Rose chuckled. "Very smart and over the top, as usual."

The hotel wasn't old, but it wasn't modern either.

Faded grandeur, thought Rose as they entered the lobby. The carpets were worn, there were photographs of celebrities on the walls and the lights were chandeliers.

There was a tall rubber plant in one corner and when they looked into the dining room the tables were covered with pristine white tablecloths.

Large leather sofas lined the walls of the lobby, with low coffee tables and vases of imitation flowers.

Charles and Godfrey were seated at a table but rose together to greet their guests. Godfrey's light grey suit contrasted with the more military style of his companion, who was wearing a gold buttoned blazer with dark grey slacks and, Rose noted, very shiny black shoes.

"Drinks, ladies?" asked Charles, with a slight bow.

"A gin and tonic, thank you," answered Pat swiftly.

"I'll just have a tomato juice, please," said Rose, flushing. How was she going to get through a whole evening?

"Don't worry about them," whispered Godfrey. "Let's just enjoy the meal, shall we?"

She looked up at him gratefully. "Did you enjoy the cathedral?" she asked.

"I'm not really into buildings. I'd rather visit the gardens," he responded, "We went to a large Arboretum last week."

"That must have been beautiful this time of year."

She began to relax. She didn't have to listen to Pat pretending to be more important than she was. This wasn't going to be quite the ordeal she'd feared.

Godfrey passed her a menu. "Choose what you like," he said, conspiratorially, "It's such a change not to have to listen to Charles all the time."

"I'd like the melon, please – and the fish. I don't think I'll have room for dessert."

"I'll try the steak and ale pie," said Godfrey to the hovering waiter, and turned back to his companion.

"Now, tell me about your plans."

Rose found herself putting into words the ideas that had been swimming about in her head for months. "In the Spring I hope to drive over to Wales," she said, "Where my mother's family come from," and she showed him the gold bracelet that she had pushed high up her arm under her sleeves.

"That looks like a valuable item," remarked Godfrey. "Two different gold colours making a tree of life design. Could it be Welsh?"

"I think it might be. If I get to see where they mined it I might find out for sure."

"I wouldn't let Charles see it. He might try to buy it."

Charles and Pat were sitting, their heads close together, with Charles talking earnestly and Pat gazing at him, apparently entranced.

Rose tried to overhear the conversation but all she heard was the word *hotels*.

That must be what they have in common, she thought, and turned her attention to her meal. They finished with coffee and Pat excused herself for a cigarette.

"We're going to Scotland next week," said Charles. "Have you been there?"

"No. We haven't been far at all," Rose replied. "We're just getting used to all the driving."

"Pat tells me she used to have interests in a hotel or two," he continued. "She must have been the perfect landlady."

"Oh, yes. She was very popular." (What had Pat told him?)

"I have a large chain of holiday properties," Charles went on, "We are expanding all the time."

"Really? (What does one say to that?) Are they all in this country?"

"Oh no – Cyprus, Malta, the Canaries. You must

come for a holiday one year. How about Majorca?"

"That's a bit far for me." She was relieved to see Pat returning.

"The taxi is here, Rose," she said. "I'm afraid we must leave you, gentlemen. It's been a lovely evening."

"You'll let me know, then, Pat?" said Charles, looking concerned.

"Of course. I've got your number."

Only Rose saw the smirk on Pat's face as she turned away.

"Goodnight, Rose," said Godfrey. "I hope you find what you're looking for."

*

"There's another card from your Nan," called Katie. "It's a picture of a castle."

She passed it round the breakfast table. "Read it out, Heather, there's a love."

Dear family, read Heather, *We enjoyed Canterbury and had a real treat. Pat nearly invested in a timeshare but resisted. This is near where the battle of Hastings took place and there is a priory and a museum not far away. We are staying here for a few days and then coming home along the coast. We are looking forward to driving over Beachy Head (not into the sea!) Love to all, Nan.*

"You'd better ring Stephen and find out about the new television," said Katie. "It sounds like they'll be back by the weekend."

Heather phoned Stephen as soon as she finished her breakfast.

"I was going to tell you at college," he said. "We have

the TV for your aunt. When can we put it in?"

"That's great, Steve. I'll tell Mum. She'll probably want to come down and supervise."

"Sorry about this, Heather."

"No problem. What's the cost?"

"We'll talk about that when I see you. Make it soon."

"OK. It'll have to be this week."

"How did your friend get hold of one so fast?" asked Katie suspiciously when Heather gave her the news.

"He didn't say. I think it's from someone he met at the gym. It won't be illegal, I'm sure."

"Well tell him we'll see him tonight – the sooner we find out, the better."

When Katie drove Heather to the flat a plain white van was stationed outside.

Stephen jumped out of the passenger seat and waited while the driver came round to open the rear doors.

Heather stared. The man was even taller than her father – with a light brown crew cut, high cheekbones and almost almond eyes.

She forced herself to look away and pay attention to the box that was being unloaded.

"I'll unlock," said Katie, leading them up the stairs.

"What's his name?" whispered Heather, following behind the boys.

"Flint," answered Stephen. "I'll introduce you upstairs – here, hold this." He handed her a small package.

It must be the instructions, she thought. It couldn't be stolen. Where had it come from? she wondered.

Once the remains of the old television had been removed and the new one put in its place Flint plugged it in and began to adjust it.

"The whole building is on Sky," Katie said. "It should be fine."

To Heather's surprise it was – and the 32inch screen was a definite improvement on Pat's old model.

"You've done well," was Katie's reaction. "Coffee, anyone?"

"Yes, please," answered Stephen. "Mrs Longman, this is Flint. Flint, this is Heather and her mother."

Flint held out his hand to Katie. "You've got a nice one there," he said, ambiguously.

"Where did it come from?" Katie's question was blunt.

"Flint is a removal man and part-time bailiff. He knows when things are going up for sale. We got it really cheap, Mrs Longman. It's all above board."

"I hope Heather contributed."

"I will," said Heather. "I do hope Pat likes it."

"What's not to like?" said Flint, gruffly.

Heather found herself staring at him again. He was wearing a leather jacket and dark blue jeans, with heavy suede boots. His shoulders looked muscular and he oozed confidence as he eased himself into the one arm chair and reached out to place his mug on the coffee table. For a big man his movements were surprisingly graceful, even cat-like. Heather was fascinated.

"Will you, Heather?" asked her mother and she realised she hadn't heard the continuing conversation.

"Will I what?"

"Will you tell Pat – or do you want me to break the news?" her mother repeated.

"I'll tell her – but when you're there, please."

"You're lucky there was no more damage. Still, at least I've met you, Stephen. Something good has come out of it."

"It was all my fault, Mrs Longman. Heather just wanted me to have a good birthday."

"Well' she knows now not to be so deceitful."

"Mum!" Heather objected. Her mother was making her look like an infant - in front of someone who was at least twenty.

"When's your birthday, Flint?" she asked.

"November – but I don't go in for parties. I like to take off somewhere. Last year I went to Holland with a bunch of mates."

Heather didn't know how to respond. If she'd said what she was thinking-*I've never been abroad,* she'd have looked even more of a child.

"Well, if you've finished we'll get back," Katie said. "Thanks again, boys."

"Nice meeting you, Mrs Longman," said Stephen as Heather took the mugs into the kitchen.

The van had gone by the time Katie had locked up and Heather sat silent in the car as they drove back to The Meadows.

How could she see Flint again? All she knew was that he used the same gym as Stephen – but if she went when her boyfriend was there would Flint realise that she was interested? She had to get to know him. Was he single? Could he find her attractive? She shut her eyes and saw his face imprinted in her memory, a face she could hardly wait to see once more.

It was after lunch on Saturday when the motorhome pulled up to 10 The Meadows. Bernard and Robbie were out, but Heather saw Pat and Rose coming from her bedroom window and called out to her mother,

"They're here!"

Katie ran to the front door to greet the travellers. "Come in, come in. Did you have a good journey? Heather, take the coats. You look well, Mum. Would you like a cup of tea?"

"In a minute, love. Let's sit down somewhere comfy. I'm not as well padded as Pat."

"I said I'd do the last bit if you were tired," retorted Pat, but she had a smile on her face. "You stay in the warm. I'll get the stuff out of the van."

She returned loaded with parcels. "Now, don't argue. We had great fun choosing these. There's something for everyone."

"Well then, let's wait until after tea and open them together. You might not feel so generous after you've heard our news." Katie stood in the doorway.

Heather tried to make herself smaller, huddling in the corner. How would Pat react? She looked so happy now. Had Heather ruined their relationship for ever?

"You know you left the keys of the flat with me for safe keeping?" began Katie.

"Oh, don't say you lost them!" cried Pat.

"No. Nothing like that – but Heather did borrow them. She had a few friends round." Katie paused and looked over at Heather.

Pat stared at Heather as if she didn't know what to say.

"Is the flat damaged?" asked Rose.

It was Heather who replied. "No – but there's a new TV. The old one was knocked over. I'm so sorry Pat."

"Does it work?" Pat found her voice at last.

"Yes," replied Heather. "We put all your ornaments away and got them out after everyone had gone. It wasn't a wild party and I'll never do it again."

"I would have said yes if you'd asked me," said Pat. "I know what it's like to be young and have nowhere to go."

"Auntie Pat – you are wonderful," said Heather gleefully, flinging herself at her aunt and hugging her.

"As long as nothing is missing. I'll just pop back and have a check and see you all tonight. Is that all right, Rose?"

Rose nodded. She looked as if she wanted to say something but was holding her tongue.

She's disappointed in me, thought Heather.

"Cheer up, Heather, All's well that ends well," chirruped Pat as she returned to the van and drove off.

"Dad – Can I go round to Naz's tonight?" asked Robbie as Bernard came out of the garden centre.

"If your mother says it's OK," replied his father. "What are you going to do?"

"He's got a Wii. We can play all sorts of games on it."

"Is that a computer game?"

"Sort of. You play it on a television. Can we get one for Christmas?"

"Maybe. Look, your Nan's van is back."

They hurried to the back door and arrived in the kitchen just as Katie was dropping spaghetti into a pan of boiling water.

"I smell garlic bread," said Robbie.

"Yes. Nan and Pat are here for tea, and they have some surprises. Get cleaned up. I'm dishing up soon."

Bernard watched while the gifts were being distributed. Heather had a set of aromatherapy oils.

"They're all natural perfumes," said Rose. "I hope you like them."

"It's a wicked present, Nan," responded Heather.

"We've brought these for you," said Pat, handing Katie a bottle of mead and a jar of honey, "all from Kent."

Robbie was given a DVD of apes and chimpanzees from a wildlife park where they bred endangered species and, finally, Bernard was handed a flat, square parcel.

"It's a book," said Pat, unnecessarily. "Castles of Kent. We hoped you'd like it."

Bernard opened it and stared at the pictures. The full page photographs of castles fascinated him. He hadn't realised there were so many, with different shapes and sizes. He knew now what he wanted to put on his tiles –a castle tower, like the one with a long name beginning with R. He might even try making tiled tables like they had at college. Why hadn't he thought of it before?

"That's Rochester, Dad," said Heather, looking over his shoulder.

He turned the page to the picture of a moated castle. It reminded him of the stories his mother had told him as a child – stories of knights and princesses, dragons and magic. He'd told Heather some of them when she was little but not Robbie. It was too late now to tell him fairy stories. That was no preparation for the modern world.

"Thank you, Pat, Rose," he said, wanting nothing more than to take the book away and study it somewhere, alone.

"Can I go and show Naz my DVD?" asked Robbie.

"If you're back by nine thirty," answered his mother.

Bernard smiled. Things had turned out just right for his son.

Heather was trying to work out how long it would take her to walk to the tennis club. It was pouring with rain and she hadn't arranged to see Stephen but Sunday was dragging. She suspected that the gym Flint used was the one at the club, although she couldn't imagine that he played tennis.

"Mum, could you run me down to the tennis club this afternoon, please?"

"Why's that? Is Stephen playing?"

"I'm not sure. I thought I might join."

"But you don't like ball sports."

"I thought I might try badminton. Please, Mum."

"It would do your brother good to join something," mused Katie, and Heather's heart sank.

"He wants to go ten-pin bowling," she replied. "He's been playing it at Naz's on Wii and now he wants to go back to the real thing."

"OK, we'll go together. I fancy starting my yoga classes again. I wonder if they do those?" But Heather was hardly listening. She was on her way upstairs to wash her hair – just in case she met the man she was hoping to see.

Hi Chantelle

It's so exciting. I've met an unbelievable man. He's in his early twenties. He's big and handsome and gorgeous. He's very fit. He plays squash and works out.

I joined the tennis club so that I could use their gym. I said I was interested in badminton but I'm not. Trouble is – I'd hate to play squash so I'll just have to impress him in the gym.

When he looks at me I just melt. He's got a deep voice and I think he likes me but I haven't talked to him much. I'm scared of making a fool of myself. What can I do? H.

Dear Heather,

Just be yourself. With all the exercise you do you must look good. Don't drool over him. Men hate that. Just be around. If he wants to get to know you he'll make it clear, somehow.

What about your boyfriend? Have you finished with him? He sounded nice. Chantelle.

Heather had also wondered what to do about Stephen.

She didn't want to lose his friendship. She just didn't feel that way about him. Besides – it wouldn't do any harm for Flint to see that she was attractive to someone else, even if it was a seventeen year old boy.

In fact, it was Stephen who gave her the next opportunity to see Flint.

"He's playing a big match next week," he told her. "Would you like to come with me and watch?"

Heather could hardly wait. She certainly couldn't concentrate in her lectures. Thank goodness it would soon be half term and she'd have her bike back.

Flint's squash playing was just as impressive as she'd expected. She couldn't take her eyes off him. He was so swift around the court that he seemed like a warrior rather than a sportsman.

The battle won, he vanished into the changing rooms and Heather and Stephen went down to the café to wait for him.

"That was great, Flint," gushed Stephen when his friend joined them.

"Thanks for coming, Steve," replied Flint, "and you, Heather."

He remembered my name! thought Heather, trying not to look as pleased as she felt.

"Heather's joined so she can use the gym," said Stephen. "She's a runner."

"Hurdler, now," corrected Heather, "but I don't just need to work on my legs."

"Your legs look fine to me," muttered Flint – so quietly that Stephen didn't seem to hear.

Heather blushed.

"How are you getting home?" asked Flint.

"We've got our bikes," said Stephen.

"You could put them in the van and I'll take you."

"Thanks, Flint. That would be great."

The three of them squashed into the front of Flint's van, with Heather between the two men. She felt unusually hot and held her hands in her lap, trying to make herself as small as possible.

"I'll drop you off first, Steve," said Flint. "I'm going to London tonight and Heather's is on the way."

Heather could hardly believe her luck.

"I'm trying out as a stunt man in films," Flint told her, once they were alone.

"I'd like to tell them about you – you've got just the look they would go for."

"You mean. I could be in a film?"

"Sure. I'll bring back a script and you can read it to me. Would you like that?"

"I'd love it. Thanks, Flint."

"Don't thank me yet. I'll let you know. Is this where you live?"

"Yes. I'll give you my mobile number. You were great today." There, she couldn't help herself. She sounded smitten already.

Flint gave a wry smile as he took the note. "I'll get your bike out. See you around, babe."

It was the way he said it – as if she belonged to him. How she wished she did!

She did see Flint around. They met at the gym where Heather tried to enjoy badminton but, eventually, gave up and used the static apparatus while Flint was playing squash. If it was an evening they would have a drink in the bar. At first Stephen would join them but gradually he appeared less frequently.

She was glad she didn't have to spell it out for him, but did occasionally miss their camaraderie at college.

The hours she spent away from Flint seemed a nothing kind of time. She went through life mechanically, all the time waiting until she could be with him again.

They began to meet most weekends, usually after Heather had been swimming.

He shared his house with two other single men and Heather never knew whether they would be alone or not.

Flint puzzled her. She'd asked him why he used his surname but he just shrugged and said it had always been like that. She was curious about his first name. She knew his initial was L but she didn't dare question him about it.

There were a lot of things she didn't dare do with Flint. When they were in company he would drape his arm round her and give her sudden kisses but when they were alone he would criticise her and ignore her efforts to please him. Sometimes she saw herself as a handmaiden, or an acolyte, but she was never treated as a partner or even as the woman she so wanted to be.

Was she too young? Did he have a problem he couldn't

talk to her about? Why was he so mysterious?

Every time she left him she determined to stand up to him – make him see her as an equal - and yet, when she saw him again all she could think of was to do as he requested. Then, one day, he surprised her by saying,

"I've a beach hut along the front. The last one in the row. It's pale blue and would make an ideal place for a photo shoot. That part you read last week, the au pair – I'd like you to learn it to do an audition. We could ask Steve to come and record it and I'll take it up to the film company."

"You really think they may like it?"

"There's no harm in trying. Steve says you are very photogenic."

Heather was overjoyed. It was the nearest thing to a compliment she'd ever had from Flint.

"Can you make it next Sunday - about 9a.m?" he asked.

"Of course. What shall I wear?"

"I'll leave that up to you. Don't be late."

7

It was a bright autumn day when Heather wheeled her bicycle across the pebbles to the little blue hut.

She paused outside. She could hear angry voices. Was Stephen more upset than she had imagined because she'd been seeing Flint? He hadn't said anything at college. She knocked tentatively at the door and Flint opened it. He waved her to a chair at the back of the hut. It didn't feel much like a film set. The walls were bare wood, the furniture a table, a chair and a bed or trunk covered with a thick, fringed cloth.

"Take your coat off," ordered Flint.

"Hallo, Steve," she said, trying not to feel intimidated.

Her friend was standing in the corner with his back to her, fiddling with his camcorder.

"It will be better with the door open," he remarked. "More natural light."

"Open it, then," snapped Flint.

Heather looked from one to the other. The atmosphere was tense. She didn't know how to break the mood. The words she'd memorised seemed to fade as she perched on the chair, trying to smile.

"Remember," said Flint curtly. "You're being interviewed for the post. Don't look pleased, look nervous."

That's easy, thought Heather. You two look as if I only just stopped you coming to blows.

"*I have my references here, Sir,*" she began, "*My last*

post was with two children aged three and one. The family moved abroad."

"Look up," shouted Flint. "Look at me! Did you get that, Steve?"

"Yes, but it was too quiet. Can we do it again, louder, please?"

Heather did it again, then repeated it standing up, then with Flint in the picture, looking down at her while she pleaded for the job.

At last he seemed satisfied and Heather expected him to dismiss Stephen but instead he said, "That's that, then. I've got to see someone else now – I'll have it when you've edited it, Steve."

He almost hustled the two of them out of the door and shut it without a word to Heather.

"He says he'll show someone in films, then?" said Stephen as they pushed their bikes up the cobbles.

"I don't suppose it will come to anything." Heather was dismissive. "He seemed cross."

"I upset him," replied Stephen. "It wasn't anything. Let's get a burger."

"You know I don't eat meat anymore."

"You can have a veggie or a fish one. I'm hungry. Are you coming to the tennis club firework party?"

"I was going to." She'd been waiting to see if Flint invited her but he'd said nothing.

"Don't expect Flint to be there. He's off on one of his birthday jaunts - Germany, I think."

"Did he ask you to go?" Was that what the row was about?

Stephen paused, as if he was wondering how to reply. Then he gave a shrug.

"I've got better things to do," was the reply.

Two weeks later Heather had a phone call from Flint.

"They liked your audition," he said. "They said you had screen presence. Can you come over on Sunday? I have a new script they'd like you to try."

Heather's heart leapt. He hadn't forgotten her. He'd been working on her behalf.

"Be here on Sunday - about eleven fifteen," he commanded.

Thanks to him she might be about to be famous.

She dressed carefully in a short red jacket with a black skirt and tights. Her hair was almost down to her waist and she left it loose, the way Flint liked it.

He pulled her into the flat and, without offering her a drink, handed her the script. "It's a serious drama," he said. "A drug addict is fighting with his downtrodden girlfriend. We don't want a namby pamby accent. You have to read it like a rough, street-wise tart. You look wrong, muss your hair up a bit," and he grabbed at her head and tried to lift her hair away from her scalp.

"Ouch – does it matter what I look like, now?" she protested.

"Eliza Doolittle!" he laughed. "Go on – surprise me!"

He paced the room impatiently while she read the scene to herself. It was more dramatic than anything he'd given to her before. The stage directions had the two protagonists either side of a kitchen table. Heather suspected a knife would feature later on and began her speech hesitantly.

"Don't come near me! I never want to see you again."

"There's no passion in your voice," complained Flint. "Try to imagine you're really in danger."

He moved round the table, gripped her wrist and twisted her arm behind her.

"Now," he said, breathing heavily into her face. "Now, how do you feel?"

"That hurts, Flint. Let me go!"

"Read, read the part."

Her eyes were smarting but his face was so close. She wanted so much to make him proud of her. She twisted away from him to see the script.

"*Let me go, you ape!*" she shouted.

"Louder – struggle!" responded Flint.

"*You'll never keep me here,*" read Heather.

"*You won't go to him,*" growled Flint, taking the other part, "*I'd kill you first.*"

His mouth came down on hers in a brutal kiss and, at the same time, he lifted her off her feet and slammed her down on the floor.

She let out a shocked scream. There was a sharp pain in her shoulder. Any desire she had felt was swamped by a combination of fear and disappointment.

Flint paused, his face red, his breathing heavy. He pulled away from her and sat up. "Stop yowling," he said.

Heather was holding her arm as if it was in a sling. The pain in her shoulder was a dull throb. She hadn't realised she was crying so loudly but she could hardly believe the amount of force he had used on her. Her face was wet with tears and she knew she must look dreadful.

"You frightened me," she said, meekly.

"And you didn't like it?"

"No. I think I'd better go home."

"I might have known a little innocent like you would want to go home to Mummy. You and Steve make a right pair."

Heather struggled to her feet, just as the door opened and one of Flint's house mates entered.

"Oh, sorry Flint," he said, looking sheepish, "Just forgot my laptop."

Flint was standing with his shoulders hunched as if he was an American footballer.

"I'm going," said Heather, hoping he would apologise – but he didn't. He marched round her and opened the door.

She grabbed her coat and left, trying to shake the tears from her eyes as she reached the street.

It seemed like the end – and she had loved him so much, hadn't she?

It was only when she was back in her own room and trying to understand what had happened to her that she realised she'd kept her time with Flint secret from everyone, even Chantelle.

Had there always been some doubt in her mind about the relationship? She'd listened to his stories of the stunts he was doing for films she never heard of, she'd made coffee and sandwiches for him and his friends when they played cards or watched martial arts videos. She'd even cleared up after them and cleaned the house, something she would never have done at home, and what had she got out of it? The strong feeling that she was being displayed rather than desired. Perhaps even the invitations to try out for film parts were fiction. Perhaps Flint was just a bully, and she'd been a willing victim.

Her shoulder was still painful – at least she had an excuse not to play badminton. She would stop going to the tennis club, now. The gym at the Leisure Centre was more friendly, anyhow. She needed to tell someone what had happened. She began to e-mail Chantelle.

Hi Chantelle,

Is it getting cold where you are? Can you send a photo so I can see what you look like now?

It has all been a bit wild here. I had an OK evening at the tennis club bonfire night although when I got home Robbie was out looking for Sooty, one of our cats, because it had got scared and run off. It came back next day but none of us got much sleep.

Steve and I aren't an item any more, although we still talk.

I didn't tell you I'd been seeing Flint – the one I told you about. He said he could get me into films – but don't worry, he didn't use a casting couch. He did get me to play-act but I think it was just to make him feel big.

Anyway – it's all over now, and my virtue is still intact. I really thought he was special but he seemed to enjoy hurting me. I wonder if I'll ever meet the right person?

Not much news. College is tough. Roll on Christmas,
Love, H.

Writing to Chantelle had made her feel better. She didn't expect a reply straight away – but there was someone else she would like to talk to.

"Mum. I'm going to see Auntie Pat. Is that OK?"

"Ring her first – to make sure she's not at the White Hart," answered her mother. "I think she's working there weekends."

Heather pressed a button on her mobile.

"Yes? Pat Smith."

"Auntie Pat. It's Heather. Are you at home?"

"Yes, dear. I don't go in until six o'clock."

"Can I come and see you?"

"That would be lovely. I'll put the kettle on."

"I've been a bit of a fool," Heather began once they were settled in front of the fire.

"You aren't pregnant?"

"No, not as bad as that. I just fancied someone who didn't fancy me."

"Darling, that happens to us all."

"Yes, but now I want to do something to get rid of him, in my head, not really."

"Like the song, *I want to wash that man right out of my hair?*"

"Exactly. Auntie Pat, you know just what I mean."

"Heather, dear. I think you could start calling me Pat, now, don't you? Auntie Pat sounds so old fashioned."

"Yes, Pat." Heather giggled. "It seems a bit odd – but your idea about hair isn't. What if I have a completely new haircut? I've had this long hair all my life. Isn't it time I changed?"

"I didn't mean anything quite so drastic. It is beautiful, and very striking."

"But it makes me look young. See what I look like with it up," and she pulled her hair back and held it above her head.

"Darling, that's far too severe – but you could go to a good stylist and ask their advice. My hairdresser in town could help you. Ring me tomorrow. I'll treat you."

"Thanks, Pat. It could be your Christmas present to me."

"I don't know about that. Let's see if they can fit you in."

It was a transformed Heather who left the salon late the next afternoon. Her long hair had been styled into a fashionable bob with a side fringe that just skimmed one eye.

She couldn't help moving her head from side to side to make the hair swing and then settle back into place. She'd refused the offer of highlights. She wanted to get used to the style first – but she felt immediately that she was going to like it.

"Oh, Heather – that's so trendy," said her mother when she returned home. "Why didn't you tell me you were going for a haircut?"

"I didn't know. It was Pat's idea. Do you like it?"

"Like it? It makes you look so grown-up. Wait until Stephen sees it."

Heather didn't really want to impress Stephen. The longer she spent with him the younger he seemed.

"It's going to be much easier to dry after swimming," she said, happily. "See, it's not only Robbie who can get a new hairstyle."

Bernard stared at the young woman who greeted him at the back door.

This wasn't the Heather he'd told bed-time stories to – the little girl who had played with the clown in Chantelle's shop. This was a different person altogether. This was a proud, poised, young woman, waiting for his approval.

He choked back his first instinctive, "NO." She had

to grow up, but it was frightening. She was too beautiful, too independent, too much like his father. She had that same air of secrecy – as if she knew something no-one else did – and yet there were so many dangers in the world that she might yet have to face.

That was the problem, wasn't it? He could no longer protect her. He hadn't noticed her changing from a girl to a woman but suddenly he realised what he'd lost.

"You will be careful, Heather, won't you?" he said, unable to put into words the confusion of emotions that had almost shocked him into silence.

"Dad! What a funny thing to say," she remarked. "I do look good, don't I?"

"Yes, darling, you look good," but he said it sadly as she turned away, tossing her hair like a circus pony.

"I'll be seventeen in February," she said. "Can I have driving lessons?"

"You'll get driving lessons when you can afford a car and not before," said her mother who had been standing behind her. "Now, smarty pants – you can set the table for tea."

"Everyone else calls it dinner."

"When we sit down late and have wine, that's dinner. At 6.30 it's tea."

Bernard watched Heather as she choked back a retort and muttered the words, "Old fashioned," under her breath.

"Sometimes," he heard her tell Robbie, "you just can't win in this household."

Unfortunately the weather was so bad in January that the family were snowed in much of the time.

It wasn't until almost her birthday in February that Heather returned to the Leisure Centre and her athletics training.

"Glad to see you back, madam," said Joe, the coach. "I hope you've been keeping fit."

"I haven't done much running but I've been swimming and playing badminton," replied Heather.

"Well, get changed and when you're warmed up we'll see what damage Christmas has done."

Heather felt stiff and awkward. How had she let the promise of stardom go to her head? This was what she excelled at – and she'd wasted the winter. She hadn't even gone on the long cross country run that the group did every year. In fact, she'd been indoors far too much.

Although the air felt sharp in her lungs she began to run more smoothly and was soon losing her gloomy mood.

The warm up exercises were every bit as strenuous as usual. Squats and press-ups, star jumps and sprint starts all combined to leave her puffed but happy.

"Get the hurdles out, Ginny," called the coach, "We have a new candidate for the 80 metre race."

Heather looked round. Who else was going to hurdle?

A short blonde girl she'd never seen before came to stand beside her.

"Hi," she said, "I'm Debbie."

"Have you done hurdles before?" asked Heather.

"Only at school. This is the first time I've joined a club."

"Cut the chatter, girls. We have work to do," called the coach.

The hurdles were set low and the girls were stepping over them to make sure they had the mobility for the jumps.

"Foot to bum!" shouted the coach. "It doesn't matter how fast you are if you haven't got the technique. I'll get the camera out and film you all so that you'll be able to see what you look like. Have any of you remembered anything from last year?"

One by one the athletes sailed over the two hurdles set out for practice.

"Don't bend forward," shouted the coach, "That's the men's way. You need to stay nearly upright."

"At least I didn't knock it over," said Heather, breathing heavily, "but it felt really slow."

The new girl had been inconsistent but promising. She was going to have some competition.

After the session Heather sat sullenly in the changing rooms. "I've gone backwards," she moaned to Emma. "All that work I did last year – wasted!"

"No, it wasn't. You'll soon get back to your old times. Did you get my message, about your birthday?"

"Yes. I was wondering how to have an evening without the olds. The meal at a Greek restaurant seems perfect."

"Who would come?"

"Steve and you. I'd like to ask Jack because I think he's eighteen so he can buy the booze. Kathy and Myra would be fun but they don't have boyfriends."

"Four girls and two boys? See what Steve says. If he doesn't mind that would be great."

"If anyone can't come we could ask Troy, he's harmless."

"Harmless and gormless. No- he might think one of us fancies him. Don't ask anyone you don't really know."

"Is there anyone you'd like to come?"

"Not really. It's your day. I just hope you like Greek food. There's plenty of choice. You don't have to have meat."

"Well, it's the next best thing to going to Greece, I suppose."

Heather was envious of her friends who had been abroad with their families. Emma had not only been to the Mediterranean, she had also been skiing in France.

Sitting in her bedroom, staring at the poster of the pop group JLS that Robbie had got her for Christmas, she felt, once again, that feeling of being tethered.

Her parents had given her money and Rose and Pat had chosen warm clothing, none of it very exciting. She wished her birthday wasn't so near Christmas.

The day came, and Rose brought a beautifully iced cake.

The meal out with her friends had been booked for the following day so the family gathered round to see her open her presents.

The gift from her parents was a complete surprise. It was a new watch, with a stop-watch function. It fitted her wrist perfectly and made her feel happy but ashamed. They really did want her to succeed and her mind had been elsewhere for months.

"Thank –you Mum, Dad," she said. "It's a wonderful present."

"I got you these," said Robbie, handing over a small box. "I thought you could wear them tomorrow."

The golden earrings looked like wings. She clipped them to her ears and struck a pose. "How do I look?"

"They don't really match a pink sweater," laughed her mother. "What are you wearing tomorrow?"

"Black, I bet," said Robbie and Heather gave him a severe look.

"I haven't decided – but I'll wear these, anyway.

Thanks Robbie."

Perhaps she was lucky with her family after all.

Katie wouldn't have seen the taxi if she hadn't been on her way to the bathroom just as it turned into The Meadows.

She had gone to bed, but found it impossible to sleep with Heather still out. Bernard was snoring contentedly, but she was anxious as to how the party had gone.

Standing at the top of the stairs she watched her daughter get out of the cab.

She couldn't see the driver but something gave her a lump in her throat. It was the company that Al belonged to, the man she had so nearly made a fool of herself over. That was thirteen years ago. Could he still be driving taxis?

I should have told her to use a lady taxi service, she thought. How on earth do you keep a young woman safe, these days?

Heather walked out of sight and she heard the key in the front door. Quickly Katie scuttled back to her bedroom. It would never do for her daughter to think she was spying on her. Still, she'd looked cheerful enough. Katie would have to wait until the morning to find out if the evening had been a success.

*

At last Heather had some good news to write to Chantelle.

She'd played down the feeling of freedom the night out had given her. She didn't tell her mother of the bottle of wine she'd shared with Emma. It was so much easier to put her feelings into an e-mail, and as soon as she'd finished breakfast, that is what she did.

Hi Chantelle,

Sorry it's been so long. Thanks for all the cards. I gave one to everyone I knew and they thought they were terrific. Mum went a bit quiet when she realised Granddad had painted them but Nan seemed very impressed. I think they'd like to get in touch but dare not in case it upsets Dad.

They didn't grumble at me for e-mailing you. Perhaps they'll let me come and visit sometime.

The birthday dinner was fabulous. The food was delicious, the music fantastic and we all had a good laugh. The boys loved the belly dancer and Jack had a go at Greek dancing. We girls are going to do it again – without the boys next time.

I didn't get home until 12.30 but we shared a taxi so no-one had to pick us up. The taxi driver looked at me a bit oddly when I told him my name. He nearly went up Chalk Pit Lane by mistake. Perhaps Dad used him sometime.

Anyway – I'm back in training now. There's a big competition coming up and I'm hoping to do well.

Love, H.

Rose was in a planning mood.

She had enjoyed the little trip she had made with Pat so much that she was ready now to venture further. However, seeing Pat so content with her part-time job at the pub, Rose doubted that she would accompany her on a longer quest. Besides – the journey she was about to make was personal, and could change her life for ever.

She took the gold bracelet out of its box and turned it over in her hands.

Had there ever been another like it? she wondered. How could she find out more about it? Heather would know – she was always on the computer, surfing the net.

Looking for the origins of her great grandmother's bracelet would appeal to her sense of mystery. It was such a pity her name had been Evans, Mary Evans. It was such a common name and Rose had no idea when or where she was born.

Then again, if she asked Heather the girl would want to come with her and Rose really wanted to do the search on her own. She would enquire at the jewellers in town. All she needed was somewhere to aim for. Once she was in Wales she was sure she could find all she wanted to know.

"There's a gold mine museum in mid-Wales," the jeweller told her when she enquired. "I'll get you the number – or you could go on line."

Rose sighed. She'd never felt comfortable using the computer and she really wanted to be at the actual place where the bracelet was made and, possibly, among people who were related to her, if only distantly.

It was all so long ago. Could she have an extended family in Wales that she knew nothing about? Perhaps the bracelet would help her find them.

Heather had been practising hard and was entered for her first inter-club event.

She arrived early and warmed up. Her form indoors had been exceptional but she was worried that racing against another team would feel different.

Katie, Bernard and Robbie had come to watch and were standing near the start as the competitors lined up.

Heather hopped from foot to foot on the spot and then crouched, waiting for the start.

There were six competitors and she was in lane four.

She was happy with that. The lane she didn't like was the inside lane.

Running to the first hurdle she felt unusually tense but she cleared it and settled into her stride.

She only became aware of the other runners when she felt the hurdle next to hers fall just as she passed it. The disturbance made her lose her rhythm; she found herself having to put in an extra pace before the final hurdle and she watched as the girl on the outside forged into the lead. Heather's trailing foot clipped the hurdle and she stumbled. By the time she'd found her balance two more runners had passed her.

She was fourth. She crossed the line angry and disappointed. What on earth was she doing, trying to get noticed if this was the result? She ran past the spectators to the changing rooms.

"Not bad, Heather," said the coach, as she reached the door. "Next time keep it up for the whole race!"

Next time? thought Heather. Does he really think there's going to be a next time?

"I checked your time," said Emma, barging into the room. "It was a really fast race. Pity about the last hurdle."

"Fourth!" snarled Heather. "I might as well have come last."

"Coach said you showed promise. It's only one race. Come and watch the rest."

"I will in a bit. What did my family say?"

"They just loved seeing you run. I'll tell them you'll be out in a minute."

"You were in front for nearly all the race," said Robbie when she joined them. "Did you hear us cheering?"

"Was I? Was I really that good?"

"Yes, you were," said her mother. "If that girl next to

you hadn't put you off you'd have won."

"Thanks, Mum. That makes me feel better. Look, Robbie, that's Myra at the high jump." She was ready, now, to turn her attention to her team mates.

It hadn't been such a bad day, after all.

"That was a good run," said a voice behind her. It was Debbie. She had not been entered for any of the races and Heather hadn't realised she was in the crowd.

"I should have kept my concentration," responded Heather. "Never mind, it's only the start of the season."

"It's going to be fun, racing against you," smiled Debbie.

"We're on the same side," corrected Heather.

"I know. I mean in practice. What do you do outside athletics? Are you on Facebook?"

Heather grimaced. She wasn't sure about becoming friendly with the newcomer so quickly. After all, she was going to challenge Heather's supremacy, wasn't she?

"I used to be when I was at school. I don't do it any more."

"Oh, why not? It's fun to tell everyone what you are doing."

Not when you can't believe what people say, thought Heather.

"I'm just getting a drink," she said and walked swiftly towards the cafe, hoping that Debbie would not follow her.

Once on her own Heather relaxed. She hadn't realised how tense she had become listening to Debbie. Now it all came back to her. She could recall the days when she first used the networking site – how she would come home from school and spend at least two hours a night chatting to a select bunch of friends.

Then the need to do well in her studies took over. The subjects of their conversations seemed trivial and Flint had been someone she had wanted to keep secret.

Should she go back onto a chat line? Did she even want to chat to Debbie?

Emma was the only female friend she had. She often felt left out when the other girls were giggling about messages they had exchanged. Why did she feel different? Was it because she felt she couldn't trust the people who contacted her, or was it because she was tempted to embroider the truth and was afraid of being found out?

There was no reason to feel threatened by the new girl but something made her want to hold back. Perhaps she could ask Chantelle. She felt as if she had no control over anything at the moment. Was it normal to feel this way?

8

Robbie woke before it was light. He felt as if something was very wrong but he couldn't think what it was.

He'd seen something before he came to bed, something strange. What was it?

He lay awake staring at the ceiling. The kitchen – it was something in the kitchen.

Was it the dog? They had all been concerned about her for some days. She'd been very reluctant to go out – but they'd put it down to missing his grandmother.

He suddenly realised what had been different. Although Sandy had been curled up in her bed her food was still in the bowl, untouched. If she hadn't wanted to eat there must be something seriously wrong.

He rolled off the bed and tip toed downstairs. Snapping on the kitchen light he looked first at the dog's bowl, to see if he had been right, and then bent to look under the table.

Sandy was there – but not curled up in her usual position. She was laid out stiffly, her legs straight and her body still. Without anyone being with her, she had died.

Robbie sat down on the floor. "I'm so sorry, Sandy. I'm so sorry," he wept, and ran his hand over her coat.

Now what was he to do? It was still early. Should he wake his parents? What could anyone do? She'd been old. They all knew that. She'd been so quiet for the last few days – almost invisible. How could they tell his grandmother?

He wanted to cover the dog. He knew she would go cold but he had to do something. It was no use – he had to tell someone. It was too much to take in by himself.

He climbed the stairs slowly and knocked on his parents' door.

"Dad," he whispered, "Please, Dad, it's Sandy."

He had to knock twice more before a bleary eyed Bernard came to the door.

The bedside light was on and his mother was sitting up in bed. "What's up?" she said as soon as she saw her son.

"Sandy. She's died," responded Robbie.

"She's dead? Are you sure?"

"Yes. She's all stiff. Oh, Mum, the poor old dog."

"Ned – you go down and see. We'll have to ring the vet." She leapt out of bed and started searching for clothes in the wardrobe.

Robbie followed his father down the stairs. Bernard was stroking Sandy's fur, shaking his head, but saying nothing.

"Robbie, put the kettle on. We'll have a drink and then decide what to do." His mother was taking charge as usual.

"Can we bury her in the garden?"

"No. I don't think that's allowed any more – but I think you can have your dog's ashes scattered."

"You mean, like a person?"

"Yes, they either keep the ashes or they give them to you to dispose of."

"We need to ask Nan."

"Yes. I'm sure she'll agree, but she needs to tell us where."

There was a strangled sob from Bernard as he stood

up and, opening the kitchen door, walked out into the garden.

Robbie looked at his mother. "It's hard, Mum. She's been with us for as long as I can remember."

"Here, have a cup of tea, then get dressed and wake your sister. We should all be part of the decision."

Robbie returned upstairs, dressed quickly and knocked on Heather's door.

"What is it?" called his sister.

"Come downstairs. Something's happened." He found it hard to keep saying the dog was dead. It seemed heartless, somehow – as if he had contributed in some way. He hadn't had he? He'd loved the old dog, watched her grow from a bouncy inquisitive puppy into a loyal and affectionate dog and, lately, a devoted companion.

They'd been careful to match her food with her age, kept up her regular injections and not noticed anything wrong except for the fact that she drank rather more water than usual. She'd never looked in pain. She'd just got slower and slower.

He wondered if that was how people died. They just slowed down until everything stopped. He knew about disease but although he'd seen dead birds and even, once, a dead squirrel that had obviously been run over – he hadn't witnessed the death of a family member.

His thoughts were interrupted by the sudden opening of Heather's door.

"Now what's up?" she asked.

"Sandy's dead," he said bluntly, reacting to her tone. Then, more gently, "I found her in her bed this morning. Mum's going to ring the Nan and the vet. She wants to talk about what to do next."

"Where is she – Sandy, I mean? I don't want to see her

if she looks horrible."

"We put a cover over her. Please come down. Dad's gone all funny."

"OK. You go first."

She followed him down the stairs.

"Ah, Heather, you're up," said Katie, "Good. Can you keep an eye on your father while I go and fetch your Nan. I've left a message at the vet's. Robbie – there's no reason why you shouldn't go to school. Get some breakfast inside you. Your packed lunch is in the fridge."

"Can't I stay until Nan gets here?"

"OK. I'll be as quick as I can."

The back door slammed and she was gone.

Bernard stood looking over the back fence to the woods beyond. Death made him feel useless. No matter what it was, the dog, the chickens, the old lady, Eliza, it always came back to his mother. There was an emptiness, a blank page, a failure. He'd not been there, he'd not seen her, he'd only heard about the accident later and he'd not even been present at her cremation.

He gave a deep sigh. At least he had her ashes – buried under the cherry tree. What would they do with Sandy's ashes? he wondered. That would be up to Rose.

He heard a slight sound behind him and turned to see Heather, waiting at the edge of the lawn.

"Are you OK, Dad?" she asked.

"Yes. Where's your mother?"

"She's gone to fetch Nan. Will you come inside?"

"In a minute. Thanks, love."

When he followed her into the house the only person to be seen in the kitchen was Robbie, sitting on the floor, his eyes closed as if in prayer.

Bernard patted him awkwardly on the shoulder. "I'd better get dressed if Rose is coming," he mumbled and headed for the stairs.

"Mum's told me what she wants and I agree," began Katie, once the family were sat round the kitchen table.

"I'm happy for Sandy to be cremated," said Rose, "but I think I'd like to scatter her ashes up by the chalk pit. If we take them to above where Lane's End used to be, where she used to go for walks, I think she'd like that."

"That sounds perfect, Nan, doesn't it, Robbie?" said Heather.

"Yes, I suppose so," replied her brother miserably.

"Mum's got to be here to sign forms when the vet comes," said Katie. "But you two don't have to stay. Say your goodbyes to Sandy and get off. You can't do any more now." Shoulders slumped, the two children left the room.

Katie turned to her husband. "Is that OK with you, Ned?"

"Mmm?"

"Bernard, were you listening?"

"As long as I'm there, I don't mind," he replied. "I'm going upstairs."

"He's taken it hard," murmured Rose.

"He'll get over it, Mum. Now…"

There was a ring at the doorbell. "That'll be the animal ambulance. I'll let them in."

Bernard stood at the top of the stairs and watched as the dog was transferred to the van and driven away.

He was due at the garden centre. He didn't feel like going but there was nothing to keep him here. He suddenly felt a pang of hunger and realised he could smell toast.

By the time he got downstairs Sandy's bed had been hidden away and Katie and Rose were sitting at the table.

"I've made coffee," said Katie. "You must have something before you go out."

Bernard sat down next to his mother-in-law and she put her hand over his.

"It's natural, love," she said. "She didn't suffer. We gave her a happy life."

Bernard gave her a weak smile. "I know, Rose. I can't help it. I'm sorry."

He nibbled at the buttered toast that Katie had put before him.

"Do you want me to tell them you can't come in?" she asked.

"No. I'll go. I don't feel like staying here." He shook his head, knowing that it would be some time before he'd get used to the kitchen without his faithful friend.

"I'll walk across with you," said Rose. "I need the fresh air."

Once Rose had said goodbye to Bernard she carried on up the road towards the village and then turned right, into the lane leading to the chalk pit. Before she reached it she found the gate and the faded wooden footpath sign that pointed over the hill.

She followed the path to the moss covered steps and then into the woods. There was little sign of the storm that had brought down so many trees twelve years ago.

The path was not well used and brambles tore at her trousers. She was glad her legs were protected from the patches of stinging nettles that had sprung up.

Late bluebells looked sad in the spaces between the trees, but when she reached the crest of the hill she could see over the fallen tree trunks, where Smallbridge Garden Centre was laid out in front of her. It looked neat, tidy, organised. The large glass-fronted building stood where her home, Lane's End, had been.

The slope, which had been their front lawn, was now an open plan area with raised beds of shrubs, trees and flowers. She could see terracotta pots lined up near the covered walkway and, where there had been a hedge bordering the woods there was now a high fence, painted green, to stop people getting onto the site. Her garden gate had been replaced by tall wooden gates, large enough to let delivery lorries through and, if she pushed her way to the edge of the escarpment she could just see the wall that had been built across the top of the site to stop any more erosion if there was another storm.

She turned back and looked round to see if she could see a suitable place to say farewell to the old dog.

It wasn't really quite as sad for her as it was for Robbie and Bernard. She'd been happy for Sandy to live with them once she'd moved into her mobile home. Sandy was the third dog she'd seen pass away. It was just one more signal that life had to change – one more indication that her future might be elsewhere.

She walked on towards the stile and then came across a part of the woods that seemed undisturbed. Sunlight was filtering through the branches of the trees and a large conifer stood alone, surrounded by a patch of ground unencumbered by anything other than pine needles and golden leaves blown from other trees.

There was an air of peace and calm about the little clearing. She'd go back and tell Katie she'd found the place for Sandy's ashes.

For old times' sake she continued along the path, down to the stile and along Chalk Pit Lane, turning right past her old camping site. People had been using it as a dog's exercise area. She hoped the garden centre would leave at least a small patch of grass for that purpose.

She turned into The Meadows and went round to the back door. It was wide open and her daughter was inside. The kitchen table had been pushed to one wall and Katie was on her knees, washing the floor.

"Don't say it. I've got a mop, but I'd rather do it this way," she snapped.

Rose grinned. It was just like Katie – to find some energetic task to do when she was upset. She knew her daughter would clean and scrub until she was exhausted. It seemed the only way she could get over whatever was troubling her.

"I found somewhere," Rose said, knowing that she didn't need to explain further.

"Good. I expect we'll hear in a few days," muttered Katie. "Will you stay for lunch, Mum?"

"Yes, of course. I'll stay as long as you like."

"I've got to be at the clinic at two."

"Why don't you go to work and leave me to get tea?" offered Rose.

"That would be great. I'm not sure when I'll be back but the kids will be glad to see you when they get in."

"Where are the cats, Katie?"

"I don't know." Katie took the plates and bottles off the window sill and wiped it.

"I haven't seen them today."

"They won't like this disinfectant smell."

"They can like it or lump it," retorted Katie, "I want this place clean."

Rose moved her chair into the doorway. "What did you do with Sandy's bed?"

"I put it in the shed. We could give it to a Charity Shop."

"Or use it again," said Rose.

"Oh, Mother. Do you think we want to go through this again?"

Rose didn't reply. She had a feeling both Bernard and Robbie would feel bereft without a dog in the house.

It was a subdued family that sat down for tea that evening. Nobody seemed able to voice the thoughts that were in their heads.

Finally, Heather jumped up, her meal half finished.

"I've got training tonight," she said abruptly. "I think I'll go now."

Her chair scraped on the floor as she exited the room.

"Have you got homework, Robbie?" asked his mother.

"Yes. I'll do it upstairs."

Katie glanced at her husband. He had a vacant, lost look on his face. He had eaten his tea without a comment and now took his plate to the sink and stood staring out of the kitchen window.

"What can I do, Mum?" Katie whispered to Rose.

"He needs a distraction. I know. Bernard? Why don't you e-mail Zak?"

"What?"

Bernard turned round to face them.

"Zak. Write to Zak. You remember how to do it, don't you?"

"Yes, yes I will. Thanks, Rose."

"I'm not sure he'll get it right," said Katie.

"Don't worry. If he's stuck Robbie will help him. They're good for each other."

"Are you OK, Mum?"

"Yes, dear. This has all made me even more certain of what to do next. As soon as we've said goodbye to Sandy I'm going on another trip."

"Where to, this time?"

"I'm going to Wales. I want to find out where my bracelet came from and see if we have any other relatives there. My grandmother had a brother, you know. My mother never kept in touch with that side of the family but I think I may be able to find them. Anyway, I'm going to try."

"Oh, Mum. We'll miss you."

"I know – but I need to do this. I don't know how much longer I'll be able to drive and I would like to see some more of the country. You understand, don't you, dear?"

"I felt you'd been restless ever since we left Lane's End. If there's family we don't know about it would be good to find them. Don't stay away too long, will you, Mum?"

"I'll try not to. I want to see Heather become a champion, and, hopefully, still be around for my first great grandchild!"

"You don't want much, do you?" Katie laughed, but just listening to her mother had made her feel better. Rose was looking forward, not back, something she was going to have to do if she was to keep the family content.

HELLO BERNARD
IT WAS GOOD TO GET YOUR MAIL
I HAVE BEEN IN HOSPITAL
NOW I HAVE TO LEAVE MY FLAT
I WILL SEND YOU MY NEW ADDRESS WHEN I
AM THERE
IT IS OK TO FEEL SAD
REMEMBER THE HAPPY TIMES
I'LL PHONE AT THE WEEKEND
ZAK

Bernard sat looking at the message. Although he could read some words with small letters his friend from the gardening college always wrote in capitals. Hospital was the only word he struggled to remember. It would be nice to talk to his friend again and find out why he was moving.

It turned out Zak's back was now so painful that he could not easily manage on his own.

Confined to a wheelchair, he was becoming dependent on others to help him get about and he had reluctantly agreed to go into a care home.

"It's very nice," Zak told Bernard. "Like a posh hotel – but I don't think I'll be able to visit you any more. I've had to give up my job – imagine that – retiring at fifty five, but I'm going to carry on working on line."

Bernard listened to his friend's brave words. It made him feel guilty – getting so upset about a dog when Zak had so much more to contend with. He resolved to ask Katie if they could go and visit Zak once he was settled in.

Meanwhile they had a 'funeral' to arrange.

Katie collected the ashes from the vet and they all

trooped up Stable Lane to the place Rose had chosen.

Heather had written a short poem but, at the last moment, could not read it so Katie intoned;

As we scatter your ashes beneath this tree
May your spirit, Sandy, for ever fly free.

"Thank you, Heather," said her grandmother. "That was perfect." But Bernard turned away and stared at the garden centre. Robbie walked over to him and put his arm round his waist and they stood there, in silence, until Katie gave a sigh and suggested they go to the Dog and Duck for a drink.

"What a great idea," said Rose. "I haven't been there for years."

"They've got a new landlord now," said Katie, "but it's still as cosy as ever."

9

Katie looked at herself in the mirror and was not happy with what she saw.

She remembered how slim and energetic her friend Lisa had been when they were in Durham. It was no wonder Bernard did not compliment her any more. There was Heather, fit and young, while, compared with her, Katie was a short, squat blob.

She'd seen a new exercise club advertised in the local paper. She would go along and see what it was like. If there were people like her there she would join.

If her mother wasn't going to be around she could do with some more female company.

'Fexercise' was a women-only club over a shop on the edge of town. When she climbed the stairs she found herself in a brightly lit room, filled with apparatus and reverberating to a heavy disco beat.

She wasn't at all sure this was for her.

Then she saw who was taking the class and she laughed out loud with relief. The instructor was her old friend, Tania.

The music stopped and Tania turned round and saw her standing, waiting.

"Katie." She jumped down from the podium and clasped Katie in a fierce embrace.

"I wondered what you did with yourself," said Katie, breathlessly.

"This is my job now. With Duane mostly on nights and Oliver at college I had to do something."

"You look completely different."

"Yes – not the gaudy night bird any more."

"What's Oliver doing?"

"He's training to be a motor mechanic. Can you hang around for a coffee?"

"No, sorry – I must get back – but I'm going to join – so I'll see you next week."

"Great." Tania turned back to the group. "Ready, girls?" and the music started thumping again.

Katie was lost in thought as she walked through the car park.

It seemed a lifetime ago that she had been part of Tania's group – going to Bingo and the pub quizzes. When she'd realised she was losing touch with her family she'd closed a door on that episode of her life. She was glad that Tania seemed to have moved on, too. Perhaps they had more in common than she had thought.

Reaching for her keys, she had the strangest feeling that someone was watching her. She turned round and scanned the other cars. She couldn't see anyone else but she pulled open the door and sat in the driver's seat. Her breathing was shallow and her hands were shaking. What on earth had spooked her? she wondered.

Was it seeing Tania again? That was a time in her life she had tried hard to forget. It wasn't only a fire in a Bingo Hall that she had escaped so many years ago.

There was a time when her whole marriage was in jeopardy, when another kind of fire had enveloped her, but she had resisted. Had the past come back to haunt her?

She put the key in the ignition and backed out of the parking space. No other vehicle followed and she began to relax as she turned into the traffic and headed home.

It was a pity, she thought, that the day had ended like that. She'd felt it was fate that had sent her to the exercise club. Now it had been spoilt by that one shadow over the afternoon. It was almost as if she wouldn't allow herself to have fun, didn't dare do something new.

She was being stupid, now. Once she started going regularly it would seem normal. Yet the nagging feeling remained – as if she expected to be punished for being selfish.

Once she arrived home it seemed as if everyone made demands at once.

Robbie was hungry, Heather was in a rush and Bernard had something he wanted to talk to her about.

"Can you talk while I do the vegetables?" she said to him.

"Can we go and see Zak?"

"Why? Isn't he coming at Easter?"

"No. He's moving. I think he's worse."

"Oh, Ned. I'm sorry. It wouldn't be easy for me to get away soon. Could you go on your own?"

Her husband looked surprised – and then, as the implication sank in, alarmed.

He's relied on me for so long, she thought. We've protected and cosseted him. He might be able to do much more. "I'll see if you could get there by bus or train. It would be an adventure, Ned. What do you think?"

Bernard looked completely taken aback by the idea but she could see by his face that the idea appealed to him.

There was an almost perceptible squaring of the shoulders and lifting of the chin. It seemed to her that after all the worry of the last few days she had given him something to look forward to.

"I'd really like to go, Katie," he said. "He's always been good to me."

"That's settled, then. As soon as I've worked out the transport we'll e-mail him and arrange a date. It will be a change. Goodness only knows, you need it."

Heather and the rest of the team left their mini bus at the edge of the playing field.

It was a venue that Heather had never been to before and she was extra nervous because one of the competitors had been considered for a County place.

"Don't look so worried," said Debbie as they entered the pavilion. "We'll show them. You're in top form."

Heather smiled. Perhaps the new girl wasn't so bad after all.

When they lined up she was in the outside lane. She looked at the other girls – one was jumping up and down as if she was cold. The others were poised, ready to go.

She bent down, alert, waiting for the gun. Debbie was in lane two, well away from her but she wasn't concerned – she knew she had the strength and determination to beat her. The girl to watch, if that was the right word, was in lane three.

Heather had tried to catch her eye but there was no reaction. 'Have it your own way', she thought, 'I'll show you.'

At the first hurdle she felt herself springing up and over, almost flying as she had judged the take off perfectly. It gave her renewed enthusiasm for the rest of the obstacles.

For once she didn't seem to have any fear or doubt. Her breathing was even, her body relaxed, and as she cleared the final hurdle she still felt fresh.

She raced forward, leaned, and was certain no-one had overtaken her. She was correct. She had won her first important hurdle race.

Debbie ran over to congratulate her. "That was a super run, Heather. Well done."

"Thanks, Debs." She bent to catch her breath. "I didn't see where you came."

"I wasn't last – but I'll have to improve some to be as good as you. At least I didn't knock one over."

"That did feel great." Heather could feel the triumphant smile stretching across her face. "Now I need to know my time."

The two girls went in search of the coach.

To make the day even better, theirs was the winning team and coach treated them all to fish and chips on the way home.

Heather arrived back at The Meadows bubbling with excitement.

"You should have been there, Robbie," she told her brother. "It was fantastic. There's nothing like the buzz you get from winning a race."

"Good for you," said her brother, "but Mum wants to see you. I think something's up."

"I'm sorry we missed your race," Katie began, "But I'm sure they'll be plenty more. I just wanted you both to know that Nan and Dad will be away next week."

"Where's Dad going?" asked Robbie.

"He's just taking Saturday off to see his friend Zak. He's not well."

"But he'll miss our home fixture," complained Heather. "Doesn't anyone care how I'm doing?"

"Of course we care, but other people matter too."

"And why is Nan going now?"

"She wants to find out about her gold bracelet. She's going to Wales."

"It's fine for some people," Heather grumbled, her earlier euphoria evaporating. "I'm going to e-mail Chantelle."

*

Rose got as far as Bath on the first day of her travels.

She immediately headed for the Tourist Information Centre and was directed to a handy parking spot.

The weather was fine and she determined to stay for a while and see what the area had to offer.

The next day she visited the Roman Baths and the Royal Crescent and bought postcards to send to the family. She'd tried to reach them by phone but, for some reason, had been unable to get through.

Later that evening, not wanting to eat alone in a restaurant, she cooked a salmon steak with fresh vegetables for her dinner and sat with a glass of wine to compose her card.

Dear Katie, she wrote, *You and Bernard should come here sometime. It is just like walking through a picture book. If it wasn't for the cars you'd think you were living in the past. It is very clean and welcoming and the people have been friendly and helpful. I am staying here tonight and then going on to Wales tomorrow. Love, Mum.*

She was beginning to enjoy herself. Not having to worry about anyone else was making her feel younger, lighter, more full of energy. It had been such a different day. She would sleep well that night.

Bernard's heart was racing.

Katie had found a coach that would take him straight to the town where Zak lived.

Zak had e-mailed a street map and told him what the building looked like. He knew the time he should arrive and that it was only a short walk from the coach stop – but he was still extremely nervous.

What if he got off too soon – or, worse still, went past the right stop? How would he know where to go? No-one would ever think a big man like him could get lost.

What if the traffic was so bad there was a hold up? Zak wouldn't be able to help, even if he phoned him. The whole experience made him feel sick.

"Calm down," Katie was saying. "The driver knows where you are going. Sit near the front and stop worrying. Here, take these," and she handed him a pack of sandwiches and a box of juice.

Bernard bent to kiss her. "I'll be all right once we're off," he said, not really believing it but hoping it would make her feel better.

"I'll see you tonight," she said and stood back as he climbed into the coach and sat down, waving at her through the window.

The doors closed and the vehicle moved off.

Katie felt a sharp pang of regret. Should she have gone with him? It was too late now. She hurried back to the car.

Something was flapping under the windscreen wiper.

An advert, she supposed – until she stepped nearer and found it was a daffodil. Who would put a daffodil on her car?

She looked round to see if any other vehicle had the same adornment, but hers was the only one.

"Kids!" she muttered – but once again it felt as if someone was singling her out for attention. It didn't seem threatening but she didn't like it. She didn't like it one bit!

The race was about to begin. For the first time Heather was to be in the third lane. She had earned it – she was the fastest under 18 hurdler in the competition.

Debbie had been pushing her hard and was very excited as her mother and brother were coming to watch her race.

"I've only got lane one," she said, "but I don't mind."

"It suits you, doesn't it?" said Heather. "I can see I'm going to have to go some to keep up with you."

The two girls were more relaxed in each other's company now and Heather was planning to invite Debbie home after the event.

There was a sharp wind blowing when the runners lined up, but the hurdles stayed upright and firm.

Heather had a good start but Debbie had a better one and Heather could see she was slightly in front as they reached the first hurdle.

They both cleared it and Heather tried to focus and concentrate on her own race. She knew she was stronger than her friend – she just had to block out the grunts coming from the girl behind her every time she landed.

As she lifted for the fourth hurdle she knew she had misjudged the distance. The result was inevitable. The hurdle crashed down and Heather went with it.

There was a searing pain in her shoulder as she landed on her left side and then her world went black.

Katie's phone rang just as she was smoothing scented cream onto a patient's feet.

"I'm sorry," she apologised. "I must take that. It could be an emergency."

It's Bernard, she thought. He needs help. Why did I let him go alone?

But it wasn't her husband. It was the athletics coach.

"Mrs Longman? I'm afraid there's been an accident. Heather is in hospital. She's had a fall. She's conscious but they think her leg is broken."

"Oh no. Is she all right? I'll come straight away. Which ward is she in?"

Furnished with instructions Katie quickly packed up her things and drove to the hospital. What exactly were Heather's injuries? How long would she be in hospital? Would she be able to walk, let alone run?

Her head buzzed with questions and she drove past three parking spaces before she told herself to calm down and steady herself.

I must seem in control, she thought. Heather will be worried sick. It is up to me to help her get through this.

She wove through the maze of corridors and rode the lift with visitors carrying flowers and cards. They looked as if they knew where they were going and what to expect, she thought. She wished she didn't have to do this alone.

She knew she looked flustered and concerned as she approached the nurses' station.

"Heather Longman?" she queried.

111

"Room 5, bed 3," said the nurse. "Are you her mother?"

"Yes. How is she?"

"She's awake. She'll be glad to see you. Would you like me to show you?"

"No. It's all right. I'll find my way."

She arranged her face into a smile and walked along the corridor.

Bernard looked around him at the unfamiliar High Street.

Look for the bridge over the river. Next to it is a big gate. Go through the gate and you will be on a path which will take you through the park. When you get to the other side go through the small gate and you are in my road. The houses are big, with long drives. Hamilton Lodge is the third house on the left. Ring the bell and they'll show you to my room.

River/gate/park/gate/third house – Bernard recited as he looked round for the bridge. He walked hesitantly towards the river. Where was the bridge? There were tall wrought iron gates wide open and a tree-lined path leading through neatly mown grass and attractive flower beds.

It was only when he had passed through the gates and turned to look back that he realised the bridge carried the road that he had been standing on over the river.

Happier now, he followed the path through the park. Smaller paths branched off but he stayed on the wider route until he reached the next gate. This one was closed but he unlatched it and stepped out onto the pavement beyond.

The road was wide with large trees and a grass verge on either side. The houses were hidden by tall hedges. Some had ornate gates but the third one on the left had a gravel drive and a large notice board announcing *Hamilton Lodge* with some words underneath that Bernard couldn't read.

He could hear his feet crunching on the gravel as he walked up to the front door. The entrance had white pillars and the door was glossy black. A modern looking box was set in the brickwork to one side and Bernard could see no other bell so he pressed it.

At first it seemed as if no-one had heard but after a few moments the door was pulled open by a lady in a pale blue overall. "Mr Longman?" she said, before Bernard had time to speak.

"Yes."

"Mr Portos is expecting you. Please, follow me. Have you come far?"

"Just from Sussex," he replied, trying to keep up with her.

"Here we are." Her voice was brisk. "I'm sure Mr Portos will be glad to see you," and, giving the door a sharp rap, she left.

There was a rustle from the other side of the door and Zak's face peered out.

He was sitting in his motorised chair and let Bernard push the door open while he backed into the room.

Bernard stood awkwardly, wondering how to greet his friend, until Zak held out both arms. His face was one big smile.

Bernard bent and hugged him, trying to be gentle, but feeling the genuine warmth of his friend's embrace.

"Come and sit down. I'll get you a drink in a moment. How is everyone?"

Bernard did as he was told, but, as usual, when given choices, found it difficult to answer.

Seeing his embarrassment, Zak laughed. "Katie? How

is Katie?" he began again.

"She's working hard."

"And Heather?"

"She's getting better at hurdles. She's very fast."

"And what about Robbie?"

Bernard smiled. "Robbie's helping out at the garden centre. He's grateful for that new computer program you sent. No-one else has got one like it."

"I'm sorry it wasn't suitable for you – but it has to be used by one voice. You'll have to ask if he can use it for exams."

"I don't think he'll want to do exams. He wants to work with animals."

Bernard paused. "Sandy's gone, Zak. Robbie found her. We put her ashes in the woods."

"She was pretty old, Bernard. We all have to go sometime. What would you like, tea, coffee or something stronger?"

"Tea, please."

Bernard watched while Zak filled the kettle and took out two mugs.

"Everything here is low level and handy," said Zak, "And after tea I'll show you the best thing about being here. They've got their own swimming pool, specially heated. I go in nearly every day, but I need someone with me because I have to have my skin moisturised after every session. I'm shrivelling up!" He laughed, but there was a trace of bitterness that Bernard had never heard before.

"There's biscuits in the tin, Bernard. Help yourself."

"Thanks, Zak."

Bernard looked around him. It was a large room – with a bed, a television set, a computer corner and a window with a view of a small, paved courtyard.

Zak's kitchen area was in an alcove and on the opposite side of the room was a door which Bernard supposed led to a bathroom.

"Can I use..?" he asked.

"Sure. I'm sorry. I should have shown you round first." Zak put the two mugs of tea on a tray and wheeled himself up to the table.

"How long can you stay?" he asked when Bernard returned.

"My bus goes at four o'clock," replied Bernard, "but I forgot to look for the bus stop."

"I'll come with you. I'd like to get out while I still can. It's a nice flat run. That's the other good thing about being here – having the park and river close by."

Bernard took a sip of his tea. He wondered what Zak did with himself all day, now he was no longer at work. How could he ask without offending his friend?

He had no need. Once they had finished their tea Zak seemed to brighten. He showed Bernard the pool and the dining room, took him out into the extensive gardens and explained that he was the treasurer for the local disabled club, and also helped them organise trips and speakers.

"I'm trying to get them to come to your neck of the woods," he said. "I hear Brighton has special beach buggies that mean we could get nearer the sea."

"I didn't know that," said Bernard, wishing, not for the first time, that he found it easier to read newspapers.

"I'll find it on the web and send it to you."

Zak sounded more like his old self now and Bernard was sorry his time with him was so short.

They went through the park together and Zak waited until Bernard was safely on the coach. Bernard waved furiously, hoping the strength of his response showed the depth of his feeling.

It had been an exhausting day and, although he was satisfied with the way he had managed, he couldn't help falling asleep. He slept almost all the way home.

When he saw Katie waiting at the bus stop he felt a wave of affection. He just loved to look at her, he thought – although she seemed smaller, stiffer, than he remembered and her face did not light up at the sight of him as it used to do.

He stepped down from the coach and was surprised when she put her arms round him and squeezed him tightly, burying her face in his jacket.

Then, taking his hand in hers, she pulled him into a doorway.

"Thank goodness you're back," she cried. "Something's happened."

"Robbie? Is Robbie all right?"

"It's not Robbie, it's Heather. She's in hospital."

Bernard's heart thumped. His throat closed and he couldn't speak.

"She's doing OK – but she broke her leg in a race. I said I'd take you to see her. Can you manage that?"

"Yes, yes, of course," he blurted – trying to take in all she had said. "Her leg? What have they done with her leg?"

"They've put it in plaster. They are keeping her in for the rest of the week and then she can come home, but she mustn't walk on it."

She paused, as if she had been saving up all she needed to say and now it was out she was empty.

"How was Zak?" she asked at last as they walked

towards the hospital.

Bernard tried to switch his mind from the image of Heather, injured and suffering in a hospital bed. Nothing else seemed so important, now.

"I suppose he was OK. He said he liked it there but he seemed sad."

Bernard almost tripped over the kerb as Katie whisked them across the road.

"Well, we don't want any more sad news," she said, "Just try to look positive."

How do I do that? thought Bernard. I just want to know that she's going to get better. There was a pain in his chest and he felt as if he was walking through fog.

He came to a sudden halt as Katie stopped to put her hands under a dispenser in the corridor. "It's to stop germs," she said, as he copied her, "Now rub it in."

He was beginning to sweat, now. The unfamiliar corridors, the feeling of mild panic that seemed to come from his wife – all contributed to his own distress.

He wanted to stop – catch his breath – get used to what was happening. It was all too quick, too confusing and too much for him to bear.

10

Heather shifted her weight from one buttock to the other. How could people spend all their time in bed? she thought.

She'd woken to find herself in hospital with a fuzzy head and a dull ache in her leg.

"What happened?" she asked a nurse. "How bad is it?"

"You'll be in plaster for a while," said the nurse, cheerfully, "but the break will mend. You young people soon get over this sort of thing."

"I broke my leg?"

"Yes, in two places – and you've got a bruised shoulder. The doctor isn't certain about the damage to your knee. You'll need more x-rays. How are you feeling? Do you want a drink?"

"Does my Mum know?"

"Yes. She's gone to meet your father. They'll be here soon. Use the bell if you want anything else," and she breezed away.

Heather looked round the ward at the curtained cubicles. How could she have been so stupid? Now what would she do? Could she still do athletics? Her whole life had been directed towards sport. All she had wanted to do was to be a winner and to help others to win too. She had no plan B. One accident had destroyed her whole life. Why wasn't anyone with her? How could they leave her alone?

She wanted to see the doctor – hear the worst and then, perhaps, she could come to terms with what had happened to her.

There was a flurry of activity in the far corner of the ward. A couple of nurses rushed in with a trolley and the curtains were pulled hastily round the bed.

Heather was frightened. She didn't want to be here with these sick people. She wanted to be home. She wanted to see her family and her friends. She began to cry.

Nobody seemed to notice. No-one asked her what was wrong. She tried to turn onto her pain-free side but any sort of movement made her feel dizzy. She was thirsty, she wanted a drink. Where was the bell the nurse had told her to push?

She twisted her body round to search for the alarm but stopped when she saw her mother hurrying in from the corridor.

"Mum!" she cried – holding out both arms and wincing as the pain in her shoulder increased.

"Darling! You're awake. How do you feel?"

"All bruised. They say I broke my leg."

"Yes. You fell over the hurdle – but the doctor said it will soon mend. Your father is outside. Can he come in?"

"Of course. I don't like it here, Mum."

"You won't be here for ever. They're going to let you home – but we'll have to put your bed downstairs."

"What about college?"

"There's plenty of time to sort that out. We just have to be patient. I'll tell Ned he can come in."

Heather had tried to hitch herself up into a sitting position but every movement hurt. Even her eyes hurt now and she wanted to close them. She licked her lips.

"Can I have a drink, please?" she said to her mother

when her parents returned.

"Yes, of course. I'll get some water."

She held out her hand to her father and he clasped it firmly. "Hi, Dad." She tried to smile. "Didn't think you'd find me here, did you?"

Bernard shook his head and then, lifting her hand to his lips, kissed it.

She tried to focus on his face. His eyes looked luminous and there was a frown across his forehead. How could she ever have doubted that this gentle man loved her? She felt close to tears again but sniffed and pulled herself together at the sight of her mother.

"Thanks, Mum." She took a long gulp of water. "Did the doctor tell you any more?"

"No. He just said it might itch under the plaster – but that's a good sign. He said it was a better break than some of these young tearaways who fall off their motorbikes."

"I suppose he does get a lot of those. Have you seen Joe?"

"Yes, and Emma and Debbie want to come and see you. I told them I'd let them know when you were up to it."

"Oh, one at a time, please, Mum – not together. I'd like to see Debbie – she was in the wretched race." At the word 'race' her face crumpled. "Oh, Mum – I might never race again!" The tears came thick and fast. Her whole body shook and she turned her head into the pillow.

She felt a strong hand squeezing hers. "Don't cry, Heather." It was her father.

"You'll get better. Everything will get better – just you see."

"Excuse me," came a voice from behind them. "It's time for Heather's medication."

"We'll have to go, anyway," said Katie. "We need to tell Robbie. I'll bring him tomorrow. You get some sleep, now. 'Bye, love."

'Bye,Mum, 'bye,Dad. I love you."

Robbie came home from the garden centre to an empty house.

It seemed strange, not having anyone in. He'd spent the afternoon in the pet department talking to children about the animals and making sure they handled them correctly.

He stood in the garden and called the cats. "Sooty, Sweep," but neither appeared.

When he got inside he saw the answerphone light blinking and pressed the button. It was his mother's voice.

"Hi,Robbie. I may be late. I'm meeting your father and we've got to go to the hospital. It's nothing serious. Heather fell over a hurdle. We'll tell you all about it when we get back."

He stared at the machine. When had they said they'd be back? What time had his father's bus been due? He didn't know. He wished fervently that his Nan was here.

Could he ring Pat? No-she'd be in the pub. He didn't know how long he would have to wait.

It was eight o'clock by the time Bernard and Katie arrived back at the house.

"Ned, you tell Robbie what's happened while I get us something to eat," said Katie, as soon as they got in.

"Don't do anything much," responded her husband.

"Just soup. We must have something. Robbie, did you get anything while we were out?"

"No. I just had a coke."

"Right. Go in the lounge. I'll call you when it's ready."

Robbie followed his father into the lounge and waited for him to speak. He looked tired, no, more than tired – exhausted.

"Heather fell in a race?" Robbie prompted. "Is she hurt bad?"

"She broke her leg. She's got it in plaster and she mustn't walk on it."

"When is she coming home?"

"At the end of the week – if the doctors say so. Mum says she'll have to sleep downstairs."

"It's a good job there's a loo down here, then. Can I go and see her?"

"Mum says she'll take you tomorrow. I wish Rose was here."

"Stop that!" said Katie, coming to the doorway. "We'll not tell her. She's been waiting years to find her family in Wales. We aren't spoiling it now. Your supper's ready. There's nothing else we can do tonight. We'll sort everything else out tomorrow."

The phone rang early the next morning.

"Katie? Can you hear me?"

"Mum? I can't hear you very well. It's an awful line. Where are you?"

"I'm in Wales, near the gold mine. It was a lovely journey. How's everyone?"

"Oh, bearing up, missing you. I think you'd better send us a postcard or ring again when the reception's better."

"OK, darling – as long as you're all fine."

There was a click and the line went dead. Katie had

managed not to let on. She just hoped her mother's trip was worth it and that she would understand why Katie had kept her in the dark.

Next morning Rose dressed warmly in thick trousers and a colourful sweater.

She felt obliged to take the full tour round the old mine, listening carefully to the historical facts but waiting all the time for the opportunity to see the results of the miners' work.

At last the group were shown into the shop and she had a chance to look at the jewellery that had been fashioned from the gold that had been mined there.

"Now the mine is closed we have to sell other items as well as the gold," explained the guide and, sure enough, there were books and tea towels, toys and sweets, all with a Welsh theme, but not what Rose was looking for.

She slid her bracelet down her arm and, ignoring the many assorted rings, stared at the case that held brooches and bracelets. Not one of them looked like hers.

Disappointed, she turned to the guide and showed him her treasure. "Did they ever make bracelets like this?" she queried.

"Ah – the tree of life. No, that particular design came from another mine. It's a fine example. Have you had it long?"

"It's been in my family for years. Can you show me where this other mine is?"

"Of course. There's a big wall map of all the old gold and copper mines and a booklet about them that you can purchase if you wish."

"That would be perfect."

She followed the guide into another room and looked up at the wall. She hadn't realised there had been so many mines in Wales.

"There. That's the one you want, much further north than here."

"Near Snowdon?"

"Well, nearer. Of course that one is also closed, but they still sell gold items, especially mixed ones like yours. They will be able to tell you how old it is."

"I just can't wait to find the place," murmured Rose. "If I find the place I'm sure I'll find the people."

The guide looked puzzled but he took the money she offered for the booklet and ushered her back into the main shop.

She wanted to rush out and leave straight away but she stayed for a cup of tea and a welsh cake, just to be sociable – then trotted back to her van to look at her map. Could she reach the other mine before tonight? She was determined to try.

"Robbie, I've got an appointment at four o'clock but I can pick you up at school and drop you at the hospital."

"Thanks, Mum. I'd like that."

Robbie had been finding it difficult to think of anything other than his sister all morning and had switched his phone on at lunchtime in the hope of news. Now he would be able to see for himself how injured she was.

The older pupils at the school had heard about the accident and had been pestering him for news and he'd felt stupid, not being able to tell them.

"She's in Baker Ward," said his mother as he jumped

out of the car at the entrance to the hospital. "I'll be back for you at 5.30. Be here."

"Right, Mum, thanks." He turned to go through the glass doors.

There was a café to his left and a long desk with someone seated behind it to his right. Across the room he could see a plan of the hospital with a list of ward names.

He went up to it and looked for Baker Ward. He felt himself becoming hot and anxious. If he didn't get help he knew he'd turn and run back out of the door.

The lady behind the desk came to his rescue. "Do you know where to go?" she asked.

"I'm looking for Baker Ward," he answered.

"That's on the ground floor. Follow the corridor round to the right, past the lifts and you'll see the name over the door."

"Thank you." He couldn't wait to get away from his exposed position. He felt everyone was looking at him.

Once in the corridor he realised that Baker Ward was, indeed, well signposted and had no trouble finding his sister.

"Did you bring me anything?" she said when he reached her bed.

"No, sorry. I came straight from school."

"Well, I'll tell you what I need and you'll just have to remember. I want some grapes, a pen and pad, some magazines and tell Mum I need two nightshirts, not the ones with cute kittens on them. My shoulders get cold."

"Grapes, pen and pad, nightshirts…"

"And some magazines – oh, forget them, here comes Debs – she'll know what to get."

Robbie looked up and saw a girl standing in the doorway. She was about his sister's age but nothing like her to look at. This vision had a cute nose and big brown eyes and her hair was a mass of golden curls.

Debbie came to the other side of the bed. "Hi. How are you? I've brought a box of biscuits in case the food's rubbish. I thought there'd be loads of fruit."

"There might be, if Robbie here gets his finger out. Robbie, go along to the shop and see if they've got any of the things I asked for."

Robbie couldn't wait to get out of the ward. Just being near Debbie was making him feel uncomfortable. He had a quick impression of a short leather skirt and long black boots as he rushed out of the room, hanging his head to hide his blushes.

It was only when he got outside that he realised he didn't know where to look for the shop.

He decided to follow the first person who seemed as if they knew where they were going. A young man passed him and walked to a set of lifts and pressed a button.

Robbie frowned. He didn't want to go upstairs. As he turned away from the lifts he saw it – a little shop, open to the corridor, with shelves of sweets, books and magazines. He'd surprise Heather. He'd buy a magazine that he had seen her reading. It was more difficult to find the paper and a cheap pen. He was nearly out of money. There were no grapes so he settled for a banana.

Now he had to find his way back to Baker ward. He looked at his watch. It was almost five o'clock. He wouldn't hurry. Being in the same room with his sister's friend was an ordeal he did not wish to prolong.

Heather sat back on the pillows, trying to find a cool patch.

"My hair must look a mess," she said, looking at

Debbie. "How did the race go?"

"I won, probably because the other girls were put off by your fall – sorry about that."

"Oh, at least some good came of it, then. Can you bring me some magazines, Debs? I don't trust Robbie to get the right ones."

"Sure. Just tell me what you want and I'll come back tomorrow. Dad'll bring me."

"Did he bring you today?"

"Yes. He'd do anything for me."

Heather wasn't sure she liked the smug look on her friend's face – but her attention was caught by the sight of Robbie, standing in the doorway looking sheepish.

"Come on, you. Did you find everything?"

"No. There weren't any grapes – but I got this." He handed her the banana.

"And I found paper and pen."

He placed them on the table by her side.

"What's that?" she asked.

Robbie's face broke into a grin. "I've seen you read this," he said. "It's like your name. It's the right one, isn't it?"

There was a snort of laughter from Debbie. "What a strange way of remembering."

Robbie turned beetroot and Heather gave her friend a sharp look. Of course, she'd never met her brother before and Heather didn't go round advertising his difficulties. She had been going to tease him about the banana but, instead, she just said, "Thank you, Robbie. It's all fine."

"I'm going now," he said. "Mum will be waiting," and he rushed out of the room, his head so low he nearly bumped into another departing visitor.

"Your brother's funny," said Debbie. "He's not a bit like mine."

"What's yours like, then?"

"He's mad about computers. He spends hours on his. He's really boring."

I'm getting tired of talking, thought Heather. I wish she'd go. She felt her eyes closing and struggled to stay awake.

Thankfully Debbie took the hint. "I'll come again tomorrow, shall I?"

"Yeah, thanks, Debbie." She hadn't the energy to say anything else.

Heather was woken by someone saying, "Would you like some tea?"

The trolley with the evening meal was being wheeled round the ward.

She tried to move but she seemed stuck to the sheets. She put her arms down by her sides and lifted her body. He pillow was drenched in sweat.

"Please," she called. "Can you help me sit up?"

"I'll get a nurse."

Once the back rest was adjusted and the pillows turned over she felt ready for her tea. There was a choice of sandwiches and she was left a list so that she could choose from the menu for the next day.

There was a television set on an arm over the bed and she wondered how she could operate it. There never seemed to be anyone around to ask, she thought.

She was leafing through her magazine when she became aware of another person by the bed.

"Emma!" she exclaimed. "It's nice to see you."

"Your Mum brought me. She's got some nighties and washing stuff for you. She's just parking the car."

"What's everyone saying?"

"Your fall is the main subject of conversation on the chat lines. But I need to tell you something else."

"Oh, yes what?"

"I'm in love."

"Emma! How do you know? Is it Jack?"

"Of course it's Jack. He's so special, Heather, and he says he loves me."

"You are lucky. Do your family know?"

"Not yet. We want to get engaged but I'm afraid of what my Mum will say."

"Have you…you know?"

A slow smile spread across Emma's face. "He's made me feel different, Heather. I can't explain it. Anyway, enough about me. I brought you a card and a book. I didn't know what you were allowed to eat."

"Thanks, Ems." She would have said more, but just then her mother arrived, carrying a holdall in one hand and a bottle of squash in the other.

"Has the doctor been?" she asked.

"No. At least, I don't think so. I've been asleep."

"You look better."

"It's all my visitors. Why don't you two sit down? You're making the place look untidy."

They both smiled and she was relieved. She couldn't bear to have miserable looking people standing round her bed.

Katie pulled up a chair and sat down gratefully. Fitting in her work commitments with this chauffeuring people to the hospital was exhausting. This time she'd paid to park in the car park but another time she'd look for a space in a nearby road, then she'd feel able to stay longer.

She watched Emma chatting to her daughter. She's a nice girl, thought Katie, dark where Heather was fair, but tall and slim. She'd make a good model.

"Heather says she might not run again. She will, won't she?" asked Emma.

"We haven't discussed that with the doctors yet but I don't see why not. Footballers have knocks like this all the time."

A smile spread across Heather's face.

That's better, thought Katie. It's really done her good to see her friend.

The visit over she got her ticket stamped at the machine and directed Emma to where she had parked the car.

"Look," said Emma. "There are some flowers on the bonnet."

Sure enough, tucked under the windscreen wipers was a bunch of heather.

"How odd," said the girl. "Someone must know your car. Do you think it is a present?"

"It's a very peculiar one, if it is," snapped Katie. "Here, you have it. I don't want it." She pulled the bunch roughly away from the car and handed it to Emma.

"Thank you, Mrs Longman. I don't suppose they'd like it in the ward, anyway."

"Someone's playing tricks on me," grumbled Katie, as she got into the car. "I'm getting fed up with it."

"Has it happened before?"

"Yes-and I intend to find out who it is."

"It's a bit creepy, isn't it? Perhaps it's an admirer?"

"That's enough. I don't want to talk about it. Let's get you home – and I don't want it discussed with anyone else, OK?"

"Yes, of course." Emma fell silent.

Katie was furious that someone else had seen her flustered. Didn't she have enough to contend with without some idiot annoying her like that?

Bernard and Robbie brought Heather's bed downstairs and set it up against the wall in the lounge. There was some discussion about whether she would like to face the front of the house or the garden.

"Put her where she can see the TV," commanded Katie. "We can move our chairs and the settee. If she decides she wants more peace we'll change round when she's here."

"Will her friends come to see her?" asked Robbie.

"Of course, at the weekend, if they aren't involved in another athletics match."

"Will you tell me when they are coming?"

"I can do. Does it matter?"

Robbie shrugged, but did not answer.

"Right, then. We'll get the bed made up and have some supper. I'm taking Emma again tonight. We'll have Heather home in the morning."

"She's a dreadful patient," Katie was telling Tania the following week. "First she moaned because we couldn't make the bed so that she could sit up like she did in the hospital. Then she got upset when she couldn't reach her

131

crutches to get to the toilet. She wants her meals at set times and I'm not always there. She hates being still – she always has. She's been playing brain games on her iPod but she could do with something more energetic."

"How about darts? It doesn't have to be the sharp kind. You can get ones that stick."

"She'd never be able to reach to get them off."

"Then try her with weights. I'll find some exercises. You can borrow a set from here."

"Wonderful. Thanks, Tania. She'd really appreciate that."

"Now, let's see if we can get you to relax. I won't play the music too loud."

Katie tried to block out all her concerns while she exercised but she couldn't forget the last time she was here. If she left a few minutes early might she be able to check the car park without being spotted – just in case someone was waiting for her?

Her session over , she crossed the road and stood aside to let two vehicles out and then, hugging the wall of the buildings, moved carefully round so that she could see the whole area.

There was nothing suspicious.

An elderly couple were loading their car with groceries and a young woman was weaving in between the cars, pushing a buggy.

She relaxed and moved towards her car.

Once again there was something on the windscreen. It was a plastic bag and she was tempted to rip it off and throw it away, but as she picked it up she could see it contained a photograph. It was a photograph of her.

She shuddered and took it inside the car. Sitting behind the wheel she slipped it out of the bag and stared at it.

Where was it taken – and when?

The,out of focus, building in the background looked like the supermarket and the full length picture of her showed her pushing something, probably a trolley, although it was obscured by part of a car.

It might have been a few weeks ago, she thought, as she looked quite well and happy. It was a pleasant picture – but who had taken it?

The only photographer she knew was Heather's friend, Stephen – although, these days, anyone could take photos anywhere. But who would print it and put it under her wipers? That was the question that disturbed her.

Did she have enough proof to complain of being stalked?

Probably not – but she'd put it away somewhere, just in case it escalated. Whoever it was – she'd catch them. What did they expect her to do?

Dear Katie and family,

I hope this finds you well. The gold at the museum did not match my bracelet but they told me where to go and I have found another mine. It was too late to visit when I arrived but I am in a very nice caravan park. A young woman with a baby let me in and found me a pitch. It is on a river but not far from the sea. I'll try ringing you when I have some news,
    Love, Nan.

Katie looked at the picture on the card. It was of a castle, Harlech Castle. Her mother was thinking of Bernard again.

Should she tell her mother about Heather's accident? No – she'd made the right decision. She would put her in the picture when she rang, but not before. She seemed so happy and there was little she could do if she did come back.

The phone rang and she picked it up. It was Emma.

"Does Heather still want to see me, Mrs Longman?"

"Of course, dear. You cheer her up better than anyone else."

"I just wondered. It was something someone said. I don't want to come when Debbie is there."

"I'll find out what the two of them have planned and let you know. I can come for you most evenings."

"Thanks, Mrs Longman. I'll be glad when Heather's back."

There was a shout from the other room. "Who was that, Mum?"

"It was Emma. She wants to know when you're free."

"Why didn't she ring me? Stephen's coming tonight, but I'd like to see her tomorrow."

"She seems concerned about Debbie."

"I'm seeing her at the weekend. You know that, Mum."

"I can't keep up with all these comings and goings, what with having to tell your brother whenever you are having visitors. It's all a bit of a blur."

She went into the kitchen. If Stephen was coming could she show him the photograph? Perhaps there was something about it that would give them a clue to who took it. She needed to tell someone what was happening. He seemed a strange choice but he was a sensible young man and she trusted him to be discreet. At least he wouldn't need picking up. He had his bike. She'd make some pasties. Young men were always hungry.

11

Rose woke next day to a feeling of anticipation. Somehow she just knew that this was the day all her questions would be answered.

It was a short walk to the old mine and the shop that still sold gold jewellery.

As soon as she entered she felt it was the right place.

Eagerly she took out the bracelet and held it in her hand. "I wonder if you could help me?" she began, approaching the young lady at the counter.

"Yes, of course."

"I've had this in the family for some time. Do you think it came from here?"

The assistant took it from her and turned it round in her palm. "It does look like one of our original designs," she said. "I'll get the book."

She handed back the bracelet and disappeared through a door at the rear of the shop.

When she returned it was with a large, heavy book. "I'm sure I've seen this on the web-site," she said, "but there would be more detail in here."

Sure enough, the design had been one of the experimental ones from when the idea of producing jewellery was first planned.

"Just when my grandmother might have received it." said Rose. "Do you know if anyone named Evans was working here then?"

"I'd need more time to find that out," replied the girl, "But there is a family called Evans who run the farm next to the caravan site. Perhaps they could tell you?"

"They are Evans?" Rose was delighted. "Thank you so much. I'll go and see them and come back if I don't get anywhere."

There was no answer when she knocked at the farmhouse door so, disappointed, she returned to the campsite. She needed to tell the young woman she was staying a few more days.

Inside the little shop the baby was crying in its pram and the woman was picking up a pile of boxes that had been knocked to the floor. More sobs came from a toddler who was hiding behind the counter, sucking his thumb.

"I'm so sorry," said the woman, standing up holding her back. "It isn't easy trying to keep both of them happy and run the store."

"I'm staying a bit longer," said Rose, trying to ignore the hubbub. "I need to buy a few things. I was trying to see Mr Evans but he's not there."

"My father-in-law? In the farm? He'll be out in the fields."

"You are an Evans?"

"Yes. Sarah. Can I help?" The toddler had stopped crying and she went over to soothe the baby.

Rose was picking up the remaining boxes and stacking them without thinking.

"You don't need to do that," said Sarah. "I'll just get her bottle."

Rose surveyed the shop. It had almost all the essentials,

she supposed, but not displayed in quite the way she would do it.

With the baby back in her pram and the little boy on her knee the young mother sat down at one of the tiny tables just inside the door. "Why did you want to see our family?" she said, at last.

"I think I'm a cousin," began Rose. "My mother had an uncle. I know he lived near here because my grandparents came from this area. They moved to England when the mine closed. I don't think the family approved of my grandfather."

"What was your great uncle's name?"

"I don't remember. It might have been David."

"Was his father Simeon?"

"It could have been."

"Well, if it was you've found the right family. He and Mildred had a girl and a boy.

Their son was called David. If your grandmother was called May you are definitely related to us. You must come to the farm and meet everyone."

Rose gestured towards the children. "Then these are little Evans's?"

"Yes, Rhys Junior and Leanne."

"This is so wonderful. I don't know what to say."

"Would you like to come over tonight, after the children are in bed?"

"That would be lovely. It's so nice to meet you, Sarah."

Rose suddenly felt very tired. Her whole journey had been leading to this point and now it was too much to assimilate at once. She made her purchases and scuttled back to the van. A whole family! A farming family! She couldn't have asked for more.

The large grey double fronted farmhouse was set back from the road, just past the entrance to the caravan park.

Rose hadn't noticed it before because the tiny stream that divided the two areas of land ran in a deep gulley edged by trees and bushes. A footpath ran along the public side of the stream – but a low fence edged the farm fields.

Rose was feeling nervous as she approached the house. What if they didn't like her? What if there was some dreadful family feud that had been secret for years and she had resurrected it? How old was Hugh, her cousin, and how much would he remember?

She felt the golden bangle that had brought her here. 'Bring me luck,' she whispered and rang the bell beside the door.

"I was just coming to fetch you," said Sarah, breathlessly. "Come in, cariad."

The front hall was dark and cool but the room she was ushered into was filled with evening sunlight and heavy oak furniture. There were tall bookshelves, a case full of decorated plates and an assortment of chairs. A large leather sofa took up most of one wall, a wall covered in paintings, landscapes and pictures of dogs.

At the furthest end of the room there were a set of French doors leading to a large conservatory.

"Uncle Hugh is out here," said Sarah, leading the way. "Come and meet everybody."

A long table was set for a meal and an elderly man sat in a high backed chair. The padded back and arm rests nearly enveloped his thin frame and his white hair framed a hawk-like face. Then he smiled, and the years seemed to fall away and Rose could see the family resemblance. Her mother had been quite plump, until the cancer had ravaged her body and then her face had become quite lean and bird-like.

She took the old man's frail hand and held it. "Hallo, cousin Hugh," she said.

"You are Mary's girl?" he answered, "and they called you Rose?"

"Yes, and I'm sorry we never kept in touch."

"Ah, Simeon was a hard man."

"But my grandfather was Welsh, too?"

"It wasn't Trevor he was angry with, it was your grandmother."

"Now then, that's enough, Hugh,bach," interrupted Mrs Evans. "Let's all eat first and we'll get out the photos and tell Rose about the family later."

The story that Rose heard that evening was even more dramatic than anything she could have imagined.

The young May Evans, her grandmother, had been working in the house of the mine owner whose son wanted to try to use the gold to craft jewellery.

They fell in love and he gave May the bracelet as a token of his affection. But the girl became pregnant and the family would not countenance their son marrying a servant.

May had an abortion and the disgrace of it reverberated through the Evans household. Her brother David was witness to his father's rages and was present when May was told to leave the house for ever.

She fled to the home of the minister of the chapel and then met and married Trevor Parry, a miner, who took her to England, where her husband found work in the chalk pit.

"He was a fine man, your grandfather," said Hugh, "very quiet, steady and devoted to your grandmother. Sarah, get out the pictures."

Sarah did as was requested and the three of them poured over the old albums while Rhys helped his mother clear the dishes.

"You'll have a drink, Rose?" he asked on his return. "I think this calls for a celebration, don't you?"

"Have you a sherry?" she asked.

"Yes, and elderberry wine and rosehip wine and dandelion wine." Sarah giggled.

"It's years since I had elderberry wine. I'd love to try some."

"A brandy for you, Dad?"

"Yes please, son."

Rhys went to the big oak dresser and took out the bottles.

Sarah put a small coffee table in front of the settee and brought a plate of home made shortbread biscuits from the kitchen.

"You have been busy," said Rose.

"You came on the right day," said Sarah. "Usually I don't have time to do any baking. The camp takes up so much time."

"We can't find anyone to run the shop," continued Hugh. "We can't pay full time wages because it doesn't need to be open all the time."

"It's seasonal, you see," said Sarah.

"I know," said Rose. "I used to run a small camp at home – but I had tents, not caravans. Although, for a time, there was one campervan."

"But you had a shop, like ours?"

"Yes – but my sister-in-law ran it. I just did the bookings."

"What happened to it?"

"We sold the land. It's a long story. Tell me about Simeon."

"That's him, there," Sarah pointed to a short bearded man. "And that's your grandmother May and David, Hugh's father, when they were very little."

The evening flew by and Rose felt entranced by the whole family. She was soothed by their voices and warmed by their welcome, but there was something else that made her feel drawn to them. There was a need here, a need for someone with her skills and experience. Was it possible that they would let her stay and help, even perhaps, trust her with running the camp?

Was Katie's family strong enough to carry on without her?

She hadn't felt vital to their happiness for some time. She'd been treading water, waiting for something to make her feel alive again. Was this place the answer?

She didn't dare hope – but it took a long time to fall asleep that night.

Heather had had enough of being cooped up in the house.

Emma seemed to be avoiding her, Debbie made her realise how much she missed the athletics club and Stephen was evasive about college.

She felt she was marooned on a desert island and when her mother told her she'd had a note from Heather's pastoral tutor she expected even more problems.

Joy Maplin was everything her name suggested. Her short auburn hair was cut in a boyish style and she wore dangling earrings and long tiered skirts. Behind her fashionable spectacles her eyes were heavily made up and her mouth was a scarlet streak across her heart shaped face.

Heather hadn't spoken to her a great deal during the first two terms. She'd managed the course work and been happy with her social life.

Now, when she knew the tutor was about to visit her at home, she felt nervous and concerned.

It would be days yet until her plaster was removed. Then she would need weeks of physiotherapy before she would know how well she had recovered. It could be the middle of the summer before she could plan her future.

It seemed that Joy had also reached that conclusion but, nevertheless, had come, not only to boost Heather's spirits but to set out options for her to consider before the next year began.

"The staff have been considering how you could best spend your time for the rest of the term," she said. "We felt that the Business Studies work should continue, but as you cannot do PE we wondered if you would like to sit in on the Biology lectures.

"You mean, in case I can't continue with PE next year?"

"Exactly. We feel that as you already have a good background in Biology you could easily get an A level in one year, if you started now."

"And if I was fit enough to do PE in September?"

"You could go back to that, of course."

"Could I really catch up?"

"That's what I wanted to discuss. If you are willing to try I could let you see the work the group have done so far. As soon as you can come in you can do the practical experiments."

"Well, it's got to be more interesting than Business Studies," replied Heather. "Can I let you know?"

"The sooner you decide the better. Meanwhile is there anything else the college can do for you? There are disabled facilities, you know."

"As soon as I can walk I'll be back. I don't want everyone feeling sorry for me, but I do miss them all. It should only be another week or two."

"I'll leave you a syllabus so that you can judge what is involved. We'll see you soon, then. Chin up!"

Heather sighed. How could she make a decision like that now? She was finding the Business Studies course really difficult without the other students around her. She hadn't realised how much the general discussions were helping to keep her interested. Sending in work on line was lonely and boring.

She couldn't see the relevance to her ambition. But what was her future now? She just wanted to get back to how she was. Would she ever race again? Gosh, she felt old; old and miserable.

She pushed the Biology leaflet aside and switched on the TV with the remote. Please, she thought, show something funny. I could do with a laugh.

Katie wasn't laughing either.

She'd asked Stephen if he ever went to the big supermarket. He looked puzzled by the question but answered in the negative. His house by the railway line was only a few yards from a smaller, cheaper store.

"I only asked because someone left this photo on my windscreen. I couldn't think who it could be, or why they'd done it."

She showed him the photo and he frowned. "It isn't good quality," he said. "It looks like it was printed on a home computer. You haven't had phone calls or letters, have you?"

"No, but someone left flowers. Once a daffodil and last time it was heather, at the hospital. At first I thought it was just a prank. Then I thought it might be someone who knew Heather – your friend Flint, for instance."

"Flint? That's not his style at all. He used to be a friend - he used to coach me at tennis, but he's twisted. I think he's power-mad."

"And you didn't warn Heather?"

"I tried to – but she wouldn't listen. She was besotted. One thing about Les Flint, though – once you've turned him down he leaves you alone and goes looking for his next conquest."

"Well, if it isn't him I don't know who it could be. I don't even know whether they mean me harm or just want me to guess who it is. It's wearing me down. I'm getting scared to go out. You won't tell Heather, will you?"

"Of course not. The things they are leaving are very odd. I don't think they're dangerous, but if I was you I'd try and stay in crowds."

"Don't worry, I was. Thanks, Stephen."

She didn't have any enemies that she knew of. At least they hadn't damaged her car. If only she knew who was targeting her.

Katie was driving along a country lane from the little village where she had been attending to one of her favourite customers when the car shuddered to a halt.

"Blast!" she said out loud, trying the key in vain.

A glance at the fuel gauge told her what was wrong –

but she'd filled up only two days ago. How could she have run out of petrol?

Someone's emptied my tank! She thought, and felt her teeth grind together.

She looked round to see where she was. One side of the road was wooded, but the other had a high hawthorn hedge. Leaving the car she walked back to a big farm gate. The view was magnificent – fields and hedges as far as the eye could see – but no houses. There wasn't a building in sight.

She tried to remember how far it was back to the village, or even how far to the next roadside property. She knew there was a fork in the road soon – but she couldn't remember seeing any buildings. It was a very isolated spot to break down – but she had her phone, didn't she? All she needed to do was to phone a breakdown service. They'd think she was a silly cow to have run out of petrol but she'd have to put up with that.

Just then she heard the sound of an engine. Another vehicle was coming along the road and she wasn't near her car! She ran back and stood by the boot, but the car sped past, ignoring her waving arm, as if the driver had not seen her.

She reached inside for her bag and felt for her phone. It wasn't there.

Frantic now, she emptied the contents onto the seat and scrabbled through – purse, diary, pen, keys, makeup, tissues, mints, comb. There was no phone.

Knowing all the time it was useless, she opened the case she used for her customers, hoping that, in her haste, she had put the phone in there. Then she tried her coat pockets, although she could feel they held nothing but tissues. She'd need those soon. She was beginning to cry tears of frustration. Had someone done this deliberately? she thought. If they had, they didn't know her very well. She would lock the car and walk – but which way?

It felt better to walk towards her home rather than away from it – although she couldn't remember seeing another village. There'll be another car along soon, she told herself. I'm not exactly lost in the wilderness.

Robbie crept into Heather's room to look out of the window.

A taxi drew up by the front door and he could see the top of Debbie's bubbly blonde hair.

His heart beat faster. Should he go and let her in? His mother should have been home by now. Heather could get to the front door but she wouldn't be pleased at having to do it.

The bell rang and he went slowly down the stairs, hoping that his sister would get there first. She didn't, and he was forced to open the door to her friend. Debbie was holding a large bunch of flowers. "Hi, Robbie," she said as she pushed past him – not waiting for a reply.

Robbie followed her into the lounge.

Heather was sitting in an arm chair, her crutches on the floor beside her.

"Oh, Debs," she said, "What lovely flowers. Put them in water for me, would you, Robbie?"

Robbie took the flowers into the kitchen and looked round for a vase. The flower stems were tied, and there was a little packet with them, like the ones he had seen at the garden centre. He cut it open with the kitchen scissors and put the contents in the vase, half filling it with water. Then he separated the blooms, cut the ends of some of the taller stems and arranged them in the vase.

Back in the lounge he placed the vase on the window sill and turned to retreat upstairs.

Debbie was showing Heather photos she had taken on her phone. They ignored him. He took one lingering glance at the object of his desire and went back to his room. No-one, pop star, model or film star had ever made him feel the way he did when he looked at Debbie. How old would she be when he was sixteen? – twenty? Was there any way he could impress her before then? If only she were sad he could comfort her – but she seemed so confident and full of life. All he could do was go to the next athletics meeting and support her. The team had a website. He'd look up when their next home match was.

There were giggles and laughter from downstairs. Perhaps his sister was feeling better. He hoped so.

Katie was cursing herself for losing her phone. She had a horrible feeling she'd left it in the pocket of her other coat. Now it was beginning to rain and although it was only late afternoon the sky was dark and the wind had a bite.

Was there a footpath over the Downs? she wondered. Then she wouldn't have to stay on the open road. The trees would shelter her and it would cut off quite a distance. Once she was up a height she would be able to see the sea and know where she was.

Hardly had the thought occurred to her when she spotted a wooden sign post with the words, *public footpath..* That definitely points south, she thought. I'll take it.

The path wound upwards through thick woodland and she began to slip on the uneven ground. At last the trees thinned and she found herself on an exposed hillside. Down below her she could see the lights of the town, with the sea a greeny grey in the distance.

The wind whipped her hair into her face but she didn't care. She knew where she was. She could see the chalk peeping through the wide bridleway that went from east to west and she knew if she followed it she would be almost home.

Cold but triumphant she plodded down the hill, crossing the main road and made her way up Smallbridge Lane to The Meadows.

A taxi was waiting outside her house but she was too tired to stop. She hurried round to the back door and went through the conservatory. Then, leaving her drenched coat and soiled shoes in the kitchen she searched for a towel.

She could hear voices in the lounge.

"I don't know why she has to be so coy," Debbie was saying. "Loads of us have done it and she's an idiot to think of getting engaged at her age."

"You've done it?" It was Heather's voice.

"Of course, lots of times."

"With different boys?"

"How else are you going to find the right one?"

"Did you enjoy it?"

"Sometimes. It depends how drunk they were."

"Oh, Debs. I don't think I could go with someone who was drunk."

Katie heard Debbie laugh and stormed into the room, trying to keep a hold on her temper. This was not the sort of conversation she wanted her daughter to be having.

"I think someone's waiting for you at the front door," she snapped. "I'm going to get Heather's tea now."

"It's all right, Mrs Longman. I'm just going. That'll be my Dad. Bye, Heather."

"Bye, Debs. Thanks for the flowers."

At the front door Debbie paused. "Are you OK, Mrs Longman? You look upset."

"I'm just wet, Debbie. I had to leave my car and walk home."

"Was it far?"

"About four miles, I suppose."

"What's the matter with it?"

"It's run out of petrol for some reason. I hope there isn't a leak."

"Would you like my Dad to take a look at it?"

"Would he, Debbie? It would be nice to get it back tonight."

"I'm sure he'd love to help. I'll ask him." She walked round to the driver's side and bent down to speak her father.

"He says if you show him where it is he'll take you back to the car to pick it up. He's got a spare can of petrol."

"Wonderful. I'll just get my boots and another coat. Heather, get yourself a drink and a sandwich. Tell Dad I won't be long."

She felt in the pocket of her coat for her phone. Sure enough it was there. At last things were going right.

She slipped into the front seat of the car, next to the driver and looked up to thank him.

The shock silenced her. She knew that man! Thirteen years ago Al had been her dream date. Now he looked podgy and red faced. Then he was charming, attractive and attentive.

"Hallo, Katie," he smiled and she felt an answering surge of familiarity.

"Hallo, Al. It's nice of you to come to my rescue."

"Again," he winked. "Long time, no see. Right, where are we off to?"

She settled back and gave him directions. How fortunate, she thought, that he had been at her home when she needed help. Was it fate – or design?

"Heather's nearly walking properly now, isn't she, Mrs Longman?" said Debbie.

"Yes. She's coming back to college soon, but I expect she told you that?"

"But her knee still hurts?"

"Yes. She won't be hurdling for some time yet."

"You know my Dad?"

"From a long time ago. I saw you and your brother in the children's playground when you were little."

"I remember going there. We used to go on the pitch and put, too."

"It feels like a lifetime ago," Katie mused. "Nothing's the same now."

"You had a boy, too?" It was Al's voice.

"Yes, Robbie." The baby I imagined could have been yours, thought Katie, but, thank goodness, he was nothing like him. In fact, he was so like Bernard she wondered how she could ever have been so stupid as to think otherwise.

"It's great to have one of each. Here we are." Al's voice broke into her thoughts.

He pulled up behind Katie's car and opened his door. The rain had stopped and once he'd emptied the can of petrol into her fuel tank he helped her out and escorted her to her car. His hand held her elbow as she sat down behind the wheel.

"You're still my pin-up," he whispered and gave her a cheeky grin.

Katie did not try to analyse the shiver that went through her. She'd misjudged him before. Was she about to do it again?

Suddenly she came to her senses. "Al," she shouted at his retreating back. "What do I owe you?"

"Nothing," he called back. "Put it on the slate," and with a chuckle, he climbed into the taxi and then waited while she drove away.

*

"Heather? Is your mother there?"

"No, Nan. She's gone to pick up her car. It broke down."

"Oh, dear. I suppose your father's not home yet. How are you, dear?"

"Much better. I'm going back to college next week."

"You've been ill? What was the matter?"

Heather suddenly remembered. They weren't supposed to be telling her Nan about her accident.

"I fell over, Nan. Nothing serious. Not worth telling you about."

"But you're fine now?"

"Yes. How's your holiday?"

"Very exciting. Not quite a holiday, but I found out where the bracelet came from and I found a whole family of relatives."

"When are you coming home?"

"That's what I wanted to talk to your mother about. Can you ask her to ring me when she gets in. The reception here seems to be better than where I was before."

"Righto, see you, Nan."

"Night, Heather."

She'd just about got away with that, she thought, but her Nan sounded different, somehow. Her voice was all breathless and enthusiastic as if she was holding in some special secret. Surely just finding relatives didn't make you feel like that?

Breathless and enthusiastic! Is that how someone feels when they are in love? she thought, remembering her conversation with Debbie. Did Emma and Jack feel like that? Would it ever happen to her? Not while she was hopping about like this. She hobbled into the kitchen.

"Hallo, Mum. Sorry I wasn't in when you called. Heather says you have some news."

"Yes, dear. I've traded in my mobile home for a bigger one. They have some beautiful ones here so I bought one with two bedrooms."

"Oh, Mum. Won't it be too big for you to drive?"

"I'm not going to drive any more. That's what I wanted to tell you. I'm going to stay here. I want to live here, darling. It's so like Lane's End used to be. I'm surrounded by growing things and the family have made me feel really at home."

Katie could hardly speak. What was her mother thinking of? She'd got a loving family here. How could she just give that up and go to live miles away?

"Mum. You can't," she stuttered.

"Look. I know it's a shock. I'm coming back for a week or two to get things sorted out. I can use the train. It's no further than people go on holiday. You'll understand when I tell you what else I'm doing."

"Isn't this enough!" Katie could feel the anger welling up inside her. All her life her mother had been there for her. When her father demeaned her it was Rose who supported her. How could she think of leaving them now? What did this new family have that Katie's family could not provide?

"I suppose the countryside is beautiful and everyone treats you like a prodigal," she said, bitterly.

"It isn't that. I've got a job. It's only part time- but it's what I'm used to. I'm helping to run the caravan park."

"Oh, Mother. They're taking advantage of you – at your age."

"It isn't like that." Rose sounded upset. "I'll explain when I come back. Pat is going to put me up. I'll see you then. I love you, darling."

Katie stared at the phone in her hand. Her mother had rung off – yet she still had a buzzing in her head. Her face felt hot and she needed to sit down.

She sat at the kitchen table and unclenched the fists she hadn't realised were so tight that her fingernails were piercing her palms. Trying to steady her breathing she went over in her head what her mother had told her.

She had bought a bigger home. That made sense. The other one was too cramped to live in permanently.

She was staying in Wales. That was what made Katie so angry. Yet – did she have a right to feel like that? What if her mother had met someone and remarried? Then she might have moved away. One day she was going to have to live without her mother in her life. Surely she should be pleased that Rose had found somewhere she wanted to spend her later years.

It's so far away, thought Katie. I've got so used to seeing her every day. I'm going to miss her so much.

"It hurts," she told Bernard that night. "It hurts that she doesn't want to be with us."

"We can go and see her, though?" said Bernard. "Like a holiday?"

"Yes, but it's not the same. I like having her to talk to. Oh, I can't explain."

Bernard wrapped his arms around her tightly. "You can talk to us," he said.

"Don't be sad, Katie."

She snuggled up against him – letting the warmth of him soothe her, as it had always done. "I know, I'm an ungrateful madam. I'll feel better when I've seen her and know more about this new family of hers. I'm just cross that they can give her something I can't."

"We still need you, Katie," he said.

It was the perfect response.

12

By the time Rose returned to The Meadows Heather was back at college. At home she walked with a stick but she refused to take it with her.

Katie drove her there and collected her every day but Heather was determined to get back on her bike during the summer holidays.

"I do wish you'd told me how bad it was," said her grandmother. "I would never have stayed away so long."

"Oh, no?" said Katie. "It seems to me you have fallen in love with the place."

"Not just the place, although it is beautiful in a dramatic sort of way, but the children, the way of life, everything. I have a little patio outside my mobile home with tubs of flowers and herbs and a bird feeder. You'd love it, Robbie."

"Can I come and see it, Nan?"

"I don't see why not. I can't put you all up at once, but I can sleep two at a time."

"Mum, can I go back with Nan?"

Katie felt a stab of jealousy. When would it be her turn to get away again? "If you like, as soon as school breaks up."

"Why don't you come with him, love?" said her mother. "I'm sure Bernard and Heather could look after themselves for a week."

"I..I don't know. I hadn't thought - there's Heather's leg…" Katie didn't know what to say. It was as if, suddenly, the sun had come out from behind a cloud. She hadn't told her mother how she had been harassed. Nothing else had happened since she had seen Al and, although she wasn't sure, she had begun to suspect that it could have been him.

"Go on, Mum, it would do you good," said Heather.

She looked at their eager faces. Could she leave her husband and Heather to cope? It might be the making of the girl to have to play house for a week.

"I will," she said firmly. "I hadn't realised how much I longed for a change. It's a wonderful idea."

Rose turned to her granddaughter. "And before your next term perhaps you could come with Pat."

"That's fabulous, Nan. It will be like having our own holiday home."

Katie felt her mood lifting. Whoever was pestering her, there would be no way they could reach her in Wales. Now she had something fresh to concentrate on. She needed to see for herself what had made her mother feel she could give up everything that was here and start all over again. She almost understood. She just hoped that Bernard would not think she was abandoning him, too.

The first weekend of the school holidays saw Rose, Katie and Robbie catching the train for London and their onward journey to Wales. Katie had offered to drive but Rose had refused, saying it would be more relaxing by train.

Rose had never seen her grandson so excited. His mood matched hers.

Katie's initial reaction had been as antagonistic as she had expected but as soon as she suggested the visit it changed completely. Rose wasn't sure why, but she was grateful.

Rose had been worried when she first saw her daughter. Obviously Heather's accident had been a great strain on her. Yet she trusted in Katie's inner strength.

If only she could make her see how important it was for Rose to remain in Wales. If Rose could make Katie see how the Evans family had come to rely on her and how Wales had everything that she had loved about Lane's End, she knew her daughter would understand.

Bernard had taken the news of the week away exceptionally well. It was almost as if he had been searching for a way to cheer his wife up and he was grateful to Rose for providing the solution.

Only Heather seemed a little subdued. The improvement in her mobility seemed to have stalled. In spite of a return to swimming and short rides on her bicycle she was still having pain in her knee and had refused to attend any of the athletics meetings.

She had returned to college for the last few weeks of term and found the students in the Biology group friendly and welcoming.

"I'm due to see the specialist while Mum is away," she told Debbie.

"Would you like my Dad to take you?"

"No. It's OK. Pat is going to take over chauffeuring duties." Her eyes scanned the canteen for Emma. She was sitting alone at a table, eating a sandwich.

"I'll be back in a mo." she said over her shoulder to Debbie and went over to see her old friend.

"Hi, Emma. Can I sit down?"

"Don't be a wuss. Of course you can."

"I thought you were avoiding me."

"Not you, just Debbie. She can't stand the fact that Jack and I are an item."

"She didn't fancy him, did she?"

"No. It's just me she doesn't like, and the feeling's mutual."

"Oh, Emma. I've never heard you talk like that. You've changed."

"Don't you say that, too." Emma's face began to crumple. "That's what my mother says. Why does it all have to be so difficult?"

"Hey, don't cry. Come outside and tell me all about it."

Once in the yard the story poured out of Emma – the way she and Jack had made plans for the future - how when she finished college they would both go to London – how he was saving for a ring but didn't want to get officially engaged straight away..

"Is he still a carpet fitter?" asked Heather.

"Yes. He says he can do that anywhere but it's his DJing that he loves."

"It's very expensive in London."

"That's why it is important for me to find work."

"I thought you wanted to be a teacher?"

"That'll have to wait. I'm going to try for secretarial work."

Heather thought it better to change the subject.

"How's your running?" she asked.

"Average, as usual. Debbie's doing well."

"I know. She keeps telling me."

"Do you think you'll come back, Heather?"

"Not for ages. I'm going to need another operation. I'm not allowed to kneel or jump at the moment. My leg only feels OK when I'm in the water. Why don't you come swimming with me one weekend?"

"I'd like that. I'll ask Jack. I usually spend all weekend with him."

"Well, don't go off the radar again. See you."

Heather returned to Debbie's table but her friend had gone. She finished her drink and sat, pondering. So much had changed in just a few months. Soon it would be the summer vacation and, without athletics, it promised to be the loneliest and most miserable summer she had spent for years.

Her talk with Emma had crystallised something that had been bothering her. The Sports Science course had been for one year only. She had the opportunity to do a different subject, even if it was only an AS level. Her tutor had suggested Psychology.

It was something she had never considered but it seemed to complement the other subjects she was doing. She determined to have a try.

Katie and Robbie were staring at the long, white mobile home. "It's as big as a house, Nan," he said.

"Well, a bungalow, anyway," she smiled.

Katie watched him walk round, scanning the large front windows.

"There's nowhere for the driver," he said.

"No, you don't drive this one. It stays here," replied his grandmother.

"Let's see inside, Mum," said Katie.

They walked from room to room – marvelling at the light, bright feel of the place, the well equipped kitchen and the big picture window in the lounge.

"It's like a little palace, Mum," said Katie at last. "What a pity you couldn't have this nearer home."

Rose did not reply.

"Where do I sleep, Nan?" asked Robbie.

"In the room next to the bathroom. Your mother and I will have the end bedroom.

I'll just make us a cup of tea and then, perhaps, we can have a walk round."

"They don't want you back in the shop, then?" Katie sounded sharp.

"I'm only there in the mornings, when Sarah has to look after the little ones. Wait until you meet them. They're such a nice family."

Katie had to admit the atmosphere in the farmhouse was as welcoming as her mother had described. Seeing Sarah with the children reminded her of when Heather and Robbie were little and she found herself on the floor with Rhys, sliding cars down a ramp and laughing with him when they crashed at the bottom.

"It doesn't take much to make them happy, does it?" she said to Sarah.

"He likes to have someone to play with," she replied.

But it was Robbie who had found an activity which really made him happy.

Rhys had a field of sheep on the hillside and two collies he used to control them.

As soon as Robbie saw how the dogs responded to whistles and calls he wanted to learn how to do it.

"You really need your own dog," said Rhys. "But you can watch – and I'll let you have a go with Molly. She's most likely to do as you ask."

It wasn't only the dogs Robbie was entranced by. He loved the sheep, too. He loved the feel of their coats, their soft dark eyes and even the smell of their damp wool.

"Your grandfather had a sheepdog and a few sheep," said Rose that evening. "He would have loved showing you what Jenny could do."

Robbie turned to his mother, "Mum?"

"I know what you're going to ask. You've seen for yourself. These dogs need to work. They aren't pets."

"I want to be a shepherd."

"Don't be stupid. There's no money in it." Katie shut her mouth firmly and then realised, with shock, who she had sounded like. She looked at her mother, recognising by the look on her face, that Rose had heard it too, the echo of her husband, Tim.

"I meant there's no future in it," Katie corrected, meekly, "but we could ask around when we get home. Perhaps someone would let you help out."

"Thanks, Mum." Robbie gave her a fierce hug. "Can I go back to the farm now?"

Once he'd left, Katie turned to her mother. "He won't want to come home," she said.

"Now you can see what I mean."

"It seems different here. Even the news seems different."

"It's away from London. It's where local things still matter."

"All right. I give in. I can see why you want to stay, and they all say you have made some real improvements in the shop. It must be nice to be so appreciated."

"You're sounding bitter, again, sweetheart."

"I know. I'm tired. I think I'll go along by the stream and have a look at the sea. Is that OK by you, Mum?"

"Of course. This is supposed to be your holiday."

Katie walked along the beach, watching the sun set over the sea. There was no wind and the water was calm with just a gentle hiss as it fell back from the shingle.

The sky went from blue to pink and gold and orange and she wished Bernard was with her. He would have loved the colours.

What was making her so sad? Was it Heather, with her plans for University – something Katie's father had denied her, or was it Bernard, who no longer seemed to lean on her for help and advice? Was it Robbie, who seemed to be growing up so fast, or was it Rose – who didn't seem to need her any more?

It's all of them, she thought. All the people I care for. They are all becoming independent and I don't like it.

She hadn't been able to face the changes until she'd come away. Now she had to find another way – something to fill the gap that the scattering of her family was leaving in her life.

Heather was back in hospital when she had her next visit from Emma.

As soon as she entered the ward Heather knew something was wrong.

"No-one else is coming tonight, are they?" her friend asked, before she'd even sat down.

"No. What's up?"

"It's Jack. I think he's gone off me."

"Why?"

"I tried to ask him about London but he blanked me. He says he's too busy in Brighton. He doesn't seem the same with me now, Heather. He looks bored when I talk to him."

"Have you been trying to pin him down?"

"Not really. I thought we'd have more time together in the holidays but he says he has to work most nights."

"It's probably the idea of marriage. You don't think there's someone else do you?"

"I don't know. DJ's always have girls hanging around, don't they?"

"Do you want to keep him?"

"I'm not sure any more. I thought I loved him. He was funny and sexy and more laid back than anyone I'd ever met. I don't know what made him change."

"Why don't you ask him?"

"I'm afraid of what he'll say. I've really messed up, haven't I?"

No. You've still got time to try for college. Do it, anyway. If I can apply with a dodgy knee you can have a go with a dodgy boyfriend."

Emma laughed. "Thanks, Heather. You do put things in perspective."

"No problem. What are friends for?"

It was only after Emma had gone that Heather let her own problems come to the surface. The operation on the torn ligaments in her knee had cured the pain but the surgeon had told her simply that her hurdling days were over. It was what she had been expecting, but there had been a lingering hope that she could resume her chosen path.

Yet, if it hadn't been for the accident she wouldn't have met the most inspiring person in her life.

"Hi, Coral," she said when she saw the physiotherapist the next day.

"Hallo, Heather. How's it feeling?"

"Just a bit stiff."

"I'll just do some gentle massage today. It's all in the mind, you know."

"That's what the doctor said. Coral?"

"Yes?"

"What do you need to be a physio?"

"You need to be nuts."

"No, seriously."

"You mean exams? How did your Sports Science go?"

"I got an A and, you won't believe it, I'm going to do Psychology this year."

"Well, you need 3 B's at least and one will have to be Biology. It doesn't matter what the rest are. Do you fancy the job?"

"After seeing what you do, yes, I do, but don't I need some practical experience?"

"Yes. You need as much observation as possible. Look at the website. Do you have a University in mind?"

"Something a long way from here. I want to be in a big city with lots going on. I think what you've done with me is fantastic."

"There are lots more difficult cases than yours, believe me. I trained in London but there are some places up North. It's a 3 year course. The sooner you apply the better."

"Thanks, Coral. I will."

Hi Chantelle

Sorry it's been so long but I've been in hospital. I broke my leg and although it's healed I have to stop racing.

It really makes you think when you see the other patients, especially the road accidents. Some of them will never work again. At least I have a family to go home to, although Nan's buzzed off to Wales to live. If I get my first choice of University it will be nearer you. I'm going to study Physiotherapy.

H.

Dear Heather,

Sorry about your accident. I'm sure your fighting spirit will pull you through. I'm very impressed with your new choice of career. James and I would love to see you. He is on painkillers for his joints. He won't see the doctor. Perhaps you could talk some sense into him. Chantelle.

Robbie had managed to attend three athletics meetings. In two of them Debbie had won her hurdles races and he had tried to congratulate her, but she was always surrounded by boys and girls from the club and didn't seem to notice him.

He, however, had noticed the boy that came to watch her last race and stood with the man he now recognised as her father.

The boy's hair was dark with blonde streaks. His face was long, lean and sallow and his eyes were such a dark brown that they looked almost black.

"Harry! You came!" Debbie seemed ecstatic.

"Dad made me," said the boy. "He said I needed some fresh air."

"You did well, Debs," said her father.

"Yes, better than last time. I'll just go and get changed."

"That was a great race," ventured Robbie, blocking her path.

"Thanks," she muttered, without meeting his gaze.

It was no good. He needed to do something extraordinary. What could he do that would make her notice him? If it was running she admired, what sort of running could he do?

Hesitantly, he approached the coach.

"Excuse me," he said. "Do you do any other running, not on the track?"

"Sure, road racing and cross country. Would you like to try out?"

"I've done lots of walking, but not racing."

"You could join in with us next weekend and see how you get on."

"Do I need any special gear?"

"See Ginny – she's in the red, over there. She'll tell you. What's your name, son?"

"Robbie. Robert Longman."

"Longman? You're Heather's brother?"

"Yes."

"How's she doing?"

"Not bad. She's doing more swimming."

"We were sorry to lose her. Give her our regards." He gave Robbie a swift pat on the back and turned away.

Now I've done it, thought Robbie. How far was a cross country run? It sounded like it could be hard work.

There were half a dozen runners in the car park on the Downs when Robbie arrived that Saturday.

The start wasn't far from his home. He'd walked there and hoped he could get a lift back from the finish.

One tall, lanky boy greeted him but the rest ignored him. The coach gave them last minute instructions.

"Don't set off too fast," he told Robbie. "Just try to keep someone in view. We've marked the route and there's a marshal at the half way point."

Robbie set off along a wide track, trying to keep up with the slower runners. The route led through a small wood and then out into open countryside.

He could see the early leaders already a long way ahead in the distance as he ran beside a low hedge. The ground was muddy and stuck to his shoes.

As the route turned into another wooded area he glimpsed a bundle of dirty white fur in a ditch to his left. He hesitated. All his instincts told him he had to go and investigate – but if he did the other runners would get too far ahead and he would never catch up.

He stopped. The others raced past him and the decision was made. If there was an animal in trouble he had to help.

Nettles and brambles hid the ditch from sight but there was no mistaking the big woolly bundle that lay under the hedge. The sheep's eyes were open but it wasn't moving.

Robbie pushed the vegetation aside with his gloved hands and got down into the ditch. The sheep's back leg was trapped in some wire, which must have been used at one time to secure wooden fence posts. It seemed as if the animal had exhausted itself trying to get out of the ditch and Robbie suspected she might be pregnant.

Taking his mobile out of his pocket he phoned the garden centre.

"Smallbridge Garden Centre, Pet Department."

"Is Geoff there?" he asked.

"Yes, speaking."

"Geoff, what's the number for the animal rescue centre? I've found a trapped sheep up on the Downs."

"I can call them for you. Where are you?"

"At the edge of the wood – not far from the car park – near the windmill."

"We start at the hilltop – which way do we go, east or west?"

"Away from our house."

"Right, west. I'll give them your number. Keep your phone on."

"Thanks, Geoff." Robbie took off his body warmer and wrapped it around the sheep as best he could. Then he climbed out of the ditch and waited for help. There was no more he could do. The animal was too heavy for him to lift on his own and he had nothing to use to cut the wire.

It seemed an age before he saw the rescuers coming along the track, but they soon established what was wrong and swiftly removed the wire, picked off the brambles that were attached to the sheep's fleece and hauled her out of the ditch.

Once they had exchanged Robbie's jacket for blankets and foil and placed the animal in their ambulance they turned their attention to Robbie.

"We'll find which farmer she belongs to. You did well, son. What's your name?"

"Robert Longman. 10 The Meadows," replied Robbie.

"Can you get home OK?"

"Yes. It isn't far." There was no use trying to do the run now. He took his filthy jacket and trudged back down the hill.

It seemed he was not destined to impress Debbie for a while yet.

It was a strange Christmas. Rose came back two weeks before and spent a week with them but then returned to Wales.

Pat had Christmas dinner with them but seemed tired and lost without Rose.

She had put on weight and revealed that she had decided to give up her little job.

Robbie was sulking because he'd asked for a puppy and Katie had refused.

"Maybe in the summer," she'd said. "When we are more settled."

It was Katie's birthday in January and when Bernard asked her what she wanted she said, "Make it a secret. Let's go out to dinner – but don't tell me where. You choose."

Bernard was delighted. He knew exactly where they could go – Pat's pub. Pat would not be there as she only worked weekend lunchtimes but she had said the meals were very good and it was reasonably near. He would book a table at The White Hart.

Katie looked at herself in the mirror. She'd lost some weight and her hair was cut short in the style she'd always favoured.

She was wearing a new dress that Bernard hadn't seen and little gold and red earrings like tiny flowers that Robbie and Heather had bought her for her birthday.

"Which way?" she asked as they got into the car.

"Over the little bridge," said her husband. "All the way to the end junction."

"Then do we go left or right?" She was beginning to guess their destination.

"Just along here on the left."

"The White Hart?"

"Yes." He sounded triumphant. "Pat told me how good the meals were."

The White Hart on a Monday, thought Katie. Surely they can't still do quiz nights after all these years?

She parked in the car park and counted the cars. There were only four other vehicles and no sign of a taxi. She gave a sigh of relief and grabbed Bernard's arm.

"Come on, then. I'm dying to see the menu."

It was only when they had finished their main course that she realised the pub had filled up considerably.

"What do you want next?" Bernard was saying, "Something chocolate or something raspberry?"

"Chocolate profiteroles or raspberry pavlova," she said, reading the menu. "I'm quite full, Ned. I'm not sure I want either."

"You usually like chocolate."

"Are you having something?"

"I'd like that."

"Well, there's usually three – let's order one and share it. I don't want coffee. We can get that at home."

The noise from the other bar was getting louder and she could see through the open door someone was holding a microphone.

"Right, folks, let's get started. Have you all got your answer sheets? Ready for the first question?"

Not only was the quiz night still operating but who should be asking the questions but Al, the taxi driver.

Katie turned in her chair so that she had her back to the bar. The sooner they finished their meal and got out, the better.

"I know you like your exercise mat," Bernard was saying, "But I bought something else as well. I hope it's all right."

"What is it?"

Bernard took out a small box and placed it on the table

between them. "I asked Pat and I went to the shop and tried the ones she said. This was my favourite."

Katie looked at the box. It was perfume. He'd never bought her perfume before. In fact, she'd never bought perfume, either. It had always seemed like an extravagance.

The egg shaped bottle held a pale gold liquid. I hope I like it, she thought.

Tentatively she sprayed some on her wrist and bent her head to smell it.

Bernard leaned forward, a worried frown on his face.

The scent was floral, but not sickly. It had a fresh, herbal tone.

"It's lovely, Ned. What a beautiful surprise."

The look on his face made her want to kiss him but, instead, she passed the bowl of dessert over to him and reached for her coat. "I'm just going to the ladies," she said, and then realised where it was. She would have to walk through the other bar to reach it.

She pulled her arms into her sleeves and grabbed her bag. "On second thoughts, I'll wait. Will you pay? I'll be in the car."

She almost forgot the box of perfume. Swiftly, she popped it into her bag and headed for the door. It was only when she reached the car that she remembered she usually left the tip for the waitress. I'm not going back, she thought. Hurry up, Ned, please.

Bernard had just finished paying for the meal when a small man with a rather red nose stood next to him at the bar.

"Hallo," he said to Bernard. "You're not a regular here, are you? Have you come far?"

"No – just from near the garden centre."

"Great place, that. Pity they had to knock down two cottages to build it."

He was smiling and his eyes looked wide and friendly but something in his tone made Bernard hesitate. Once before he'd met someone who seemed too eager to confide in a stranger. It had led to hurt feelings all round and he didn't want that to happen again. The man looked as if he was waiting for an opening to say more. Bernard decided not to give it to him.

"I must go. My wife's waiting," he said, and turned away from his companion.

"See you again," came the over-friendly reply.

The next celebration was Heather's eighteenth birthday. She had been studying especially hard for two months, only going out to the placements her mother had found for her at local care homes. The Sports Injury Clinic had promised she could have three days of observation in the Easter holidays.

She'd sent in her applications for her chosen Universities and had told Chantelle she would try to visit her grandfather when she visited the Open Day held in the city in the north west in June.

"I don't know why you want to go so far away," grumbled her mother. "Think of the travel costs."

"It just looked an exciting place. I've also got one in Wales, but it's miles away from Nan."

Soon they'll only be Robbie at home, thought Katie, and even he wants to spend more time at the farm than he does here.

"I'm sorry we can't afford to come with you," said Katie to Heather as she was packing for her trip up north.

"It's fine, mum. I'd rather go on my own. You don't have

to worry about me. There'll be loads of other students going too."

"But they won't be going on to the Lake District."

"Mum, it's only for one night. You'd like to know how Granddad and Chantelle are doing really, wouldn't you?"

"I'm surprised they're still together."

"I don't think Granddad is very well."

"He's getting on, Heather. Don't expect too much."

"I won't. I just want to see Chantelle and let them know that I'm doing OK."

"You're lucky to have more than one offer of a place. Let's hope your results are as good as you expect."

"Mum! Don't be so negative."

"I just don't want you to be disappointed."

"This is the most exciting thing I have ever done in my life. Trust me."

Katie watched her shut the case and reach for her jacket. She's so grown up, she thought, and so much more confident than I was at her age. She felt a strange mixture of pride and envy.

Perhaps they had been too hasty, cutting themselves off from James, but it was Bernard's decision, and she had gone along with it. After all, his father had not only abandoned him when he was only seven years old – but he'd come back into his life when Heather was only four and then run away again, with Chantelle.

Just the thought of him made her angry – but she had to recognise it was always Heather that he'd been fond of and she had to admire her daughter for keeping in touch.

As soon as she'd seen Heather off at the station Katie turned towards Pat's flat.

She had grown increasingly worried about her aunt over the previous few months.

Now she was longer working, Pat didn't seem to have the energy to do anything. Her once red hair was lank and grey. Her shapely figure was now bloated and lumpy and her legs were veined and swollen.

Pat opened the door and then shuffled back to her chair, breathing heavily.

"What have you been up to, Pat?" Katie tried to sound up-beat but couldn't block out the untidy, neglected look of the room.

"Not much, dearie," Pat seemed to have difficulty speaking. "Has Heather gone?"

"Yes. I've just seen her off. What are you doing for lunch? Can I help?"

"Thanks, Katie. There's a meal in the freezer. The van brings seven a week. It just needs microwaving."

"I'll make some tea and bread and butter and join you. There's no one at home."

Pat picked at her meal and drank half a cup of tea.

How has she got so fat if this is all she eats? thought Katie.

"Would you like me to hoover round? she asked.

"No. It doesn't matter. I usually watch TV now. I like medical programmes."

"Well, let me know if I can get you anything, won't you?"

"Yes, dear. I'm fine. Thank you for coming."

Katie drove home slowly. There was one more thing she had to do which might bring more joy into the family. She was going to look at some sheepdog puppies.

If Robbie had one he would have to keep it at the farm, but it was all he seemed to care about now.

She'd write to Lisa. She would understand what it was like to have an 'empty nest.' Ryan had been posted overseas and was in much more danger than Katie's children. She supposed she should think herself lucky. Trouble was, she didn't feel it.

Heather sat at the desk in Chantelle's flat above the shop.

Hi Emma,

Chantelle let me use her computer to keep in touch. It was fabulous seeing her and granddad although he has very bad arthritis. I have given him some exercises to do that I learned from the physio in the hospital.

The University was terrific – and the city even better than I expected. The buildings are enormous and the harbour area is humming. I'm going to love it here. I met some older students and they said the night life was awesome. There's loads of societies to join. Can you see me in the debating club, or even on stage?

I hope you're over Jack. I'll be back soon and then we'll just have to keep our fingers crossed for our results.

Love, H.

Bernard had been called into the manager's office. "Bernard – there's some discrepancy in the stock. We seem to have mislaid a number of ornamental urns and statues. Have you noticed anything going missing?"

"No, sorry. If they weren't there I'd think they'd been sold."

"Well I think we'll move the display. Could you bring them inside for us, please, Bernard?"

"Sure. We'll be able to watch them better from there."

The pots and figures were heavy and Bernard's back and arms were aching by the time he had shifted them to their new position. They were displayed round an imitation pond, just outside the pet department so that if the girls on the checkout didn't see anyone tampering with them, then the assistant in the pet store might see them. The only problem Bernard could see was that they were now very near the entrance.

He sat on a bench and closed his eyes for a moment. He missed having Robbie around to help him, but his son only wanted to be with the sheep nowadays.

Although Bernard worked with other people he couldn't call them friends. Everyone was younger than him, apart from old Stan, who probably should have retired years ago, and he had little in common with any of them.

Katie had joined an exercise class. Should he do something like that? He hadn't thought about going anywhere without Katie before, not until the trip to see Zak.

The man at the pub had made him feel left out – as if there were pleasures in life that he was missing. He didn't want to go out to drink – but perhaps there was something else he could do? He'd e-mail Zak. His friend was always full of good advice.

Zak's reply, when it came, was full of encouragement.

YOU ARE FIT AND STRONG.
ASK KATIE ABOUT CLUBS. SAILING, DANCING, BOWLING?

Bernard considered what Zak had suggested. Sailing? Bernard would rather be in the water than on it. Dancing?

Definitely not. He couldn't remember steps and didn't like loud music. Bowling? Zak didn't say what kind of bowling but Bernard had watched the men in the park bowling on the green. That was the kind of bowling he would like to do. Would they let him join? he wondered. He would ask. They could only say no. He had the feeling he would be quite good at it once they had taught him the rules.

Would Katie be upset if he went to something without her? He wished Rose was around to ask. Never mind, he'd go and ask Pat instead. He'd go and see her on his day off. Now he needed to sweep up and get home. The customers had all left and the manager was waiting to close up.

There was no reply when Bernard rang the bell for Pat's flat. He waited a few moments and tried again.

Katie had a key but he hadn't thought to bring it with him. He stood outside the door, undecided.

There were footsteps behind him and an elderly lady he recognised as Pat's neighbour passed him and then stopped, looking back. "Isn't she answering?" she said.

"No," replied Bernard. "I can't get in."

"I can," said the neighbour. "I'll fetch the key. I hope she's all right."

The flat was eerily silent when they got inside. There was no smell of cooking, no sound of the television and no sign of Pat.

"Wait there," said the neighbour and opened the door to the bedroom. She closed it behind her and Bernard waited nervously until she reappeared.

"We'd better call the doctor," she said. "I think she's passed away."

"Oh." Bernard sat down suddenly and grabbed hold of the table. He took a deep breath and then stood, steadied himself and walked slowly towards the bedroom.

Opening the door a crack he peered in.

Pat was lying, fully clothed, on the bed, as if she had gone for an afternoon nap, but her face was stiff and her body still.

The neighbour was on the phone, giving the address. "Yes, we'll wait here until you come," she said and then turned to Bernard. "Bernard, would you like to call your wife?"

"Er – oh, yes. I can use my phone." Bernard tried to pull himself together. His legs felt wobbly again, and he needed a drink of water.

He went into the kitchen, took a mug from the shelf and filled it from the cold tap. A used plate and cutlery sat in the washing up bowl and an open cake tin sat on the worktop. He replaced the lid and put it in the cupboard. Then he took a large mouthful of water and phoned the number for Katie. If she was driving he knew she wouldn't answer, but if she was with a client her phone would be on.

"Yes, Ned?" she answered. "I won't be long. What is it?"

"It's Pat. I'm in her flat. She's died, Katie. She's on the bed."

Bernard heard her gasp of surprise. "Are you on your own or is someone with you?" she said.

"The neighbour's here. She's rung the doctor."

"Good. He'll sort everything out. I'll come as soon as I finish here. Keep calm, darling. Don't move anything."

Bernard looked round the kitchen. He'd already moved a mug and the cake tin. Should he get it back out? He felt guilty. Why had Katie said that? Should they call the police? He staggered back to the sitting room.

"Katie's coming," he said. "She told me not to move anything."

"She means medicines, and anything to show what she has been eating and drinking," said the neighbour, "but I bet my bottom dollar it's natural causes. I expect her heart just gave out."

Bernard felt tears come to his eyes. He didn't want to cry in front of a comparative stranger.

There was a knock at the door. "Mrs Smith's place?" said a voice.

"Yes, doctor. Come in. She's in the bedroom. This is her niece's husband. Her niece is on her way."

Bernard retreated into the background and stayed there while everyone else busied themselves with the necessary arrangements.

Katie took charge as soon as she arrived and, two hours later, was driving them both home with a box of documents in the boot and a grim look on her face.

"Now to tell Mum," she said as soon as they got inside the house. "Make us a cup of tea, will you, love? This isn't going to be easy."

Rose returned for the funeral, staying in Pat's flat, although Katie had offered to put her up at The Meadows.

It was when the solicitor informed them of the contents of Pat's will that the family were stunned.

Pat had left her flat not to Rose, but to Katie, and she had asked for the rest of the money from her estate to be divided equally between Heather and Robbie. She had also, much to the girl's delight, left her car to Heather.

"I'm so sorry, Mum," said Katie. "I don't expect she thought she'd go before you."

"I did get a letter from her about three weeks ago," said Rose. "She said if anything happened to her I was to have one of her paintings, the one of the girl on the cliff top, and all the photos of George and Tim – if I wanted them."

"You can have anything from the flat. I don't want it. I suppose I'll have to sell it."

"Don't do anything hasty. It's almost as if she was expecting the worst."

"I wonder if I could let it," mused Katie. "It's so central – but I think the lease stipulates over fifties."

"Mum, can I have driving lessons now?" interrupted Heather.

"Yes, I suppose so – but you'll have to pay for them yourself. At least the money will help with your course."

She noticed her husband, then, sitting with his head in his hands. "Don't get depressed, darling. It will get easier with time."

Bernard looked up at her. "I know. It's just that she was alone."

There was a stunned silence. He had voiced what the others had thought, but not dared to say.

"She's been very generous – we'll never forget her," said Katie at last.

13

Bernard had begun to count the statues every day when he started work and then he checked them every evening to make sure they were all there.

It meant he had to ask at the tills if they had sold any when he wasn't looking but they were not items that were purchased every day.

A week later he counted the statues as usual. The Grecian girls were all correct, the cherubs, the stone rabbits and the tortoises - but when it came to the frogs, there were two missing.

"Have you sold any frog ornaments?" he asked the sales girls.

"No, Bernard. Are there any missing?"

"Two – unless they have been moved for display."

"Ask Karen."

Bernard asked everybody, including the manager, who insisted on counting them for himself.

"It's a good job they aren't too valuable," he muttered. "I wonder how they managed it – and when. I'm going to have to restrict who has keys. You'd better give me yours, Bernard."

"But I live the nearest."

"Geoff or I will have to get here a bit earlier. If you don't have keys you can't be a suspect."

Geoff wasn't happy at having to start work earlier but Karen gave up her keys.

Bernard felt he had been unfairly stripped of a layer of authority. He'd enjoyed being the first person in and, sometimes, the last person out. It had made him feel trusted. Now the only way to regain that trust was to find out who had stolen the ornaments.

He didn't think they'd gone while the store was open. He would come out at night, he decided, and see if he could catch the thief in the act.

Katie was scathing. "How do you know they'll come back again?" she said. "What a fuss over two pot frogs. I'd understand it if they'd smashed up the place or stolen the takings."

"Geoff said they probably sold them at car boot fairs," said Bernard.

"Hey, Mum. Can we go to one and see if we can spot the loot!" said Heather.

"No. It's probably gone by now. Your father is just being too conscientious. I don't want to be woken up in the middle of the night just because you want to play detective."

"I'll sleep in Heather's bed when she goes away."

"If you must – but not for more than a week. If you don't see anything then promise me you'll stop."

"Don't they keep the lights on in the garden centre?" asked Heather.

"Just very dim. That's why you wouldn't see anyone with a torch. I'm going to hide in the trees. They need a car to take anything big."

"Two frogs aren't very big."

"I know. That's what bothers me, but bigger things have gone."

"Can I come, Dad?"

"No, Robbie. You need your sleep." It was Katie who replied in an instant, her face an angry frown.

Next day Bernard was again called into the manager's office.

On the table was a stone frog.

"You got it back?" exclaimed Bernard.

"Yes, Bernard. Geoff and I went through all the lockers and found this one."

"Where was it?"

"In your locker."

"In my locker?" Bernard couldn't believe it. "I hardly use it. I haven't looked in it for a week."

"But you have the only other key."

"Why would I put a frog in my locker?"

"I don't know. Did you?"

"No. Of course I didn't."

"Well, somebody did. It's a pretty clumsy way to incriminate you, I grant."

"I'm going to check the place at night – if you say it's OK," said Bernard.

"As long as you do it from outside. I can't give you the keys back now Geoff has seen where we found the frog."

"If I can catch the real thief will you trust me again?"

"Bernard – I don't really think it is you. I don't like to think it's anyone on the staff – but I'm going to have to consider it."

"Thanks, Mr Dunn. Shall I put the frog back on display?"

"No. I don't think so. I'll keep it here for a while in case something else happens. You get back to work."

Bernard returned to the compost and gravels section. Piles of sacks needed stacking. If he did that he might stop worrying about the stolen ornaments, and who would put one in his locker. He didn't like mysteries. Perhaps he'd find the answer one night time. He hoped so.

Heather was overjoyed. Her exam grades had been better than she had dared hope and she'd got into her first choice Uni'. She had thrown herself into preparation for her move up North. Her first year would be spent on campus, sharing a room with another student. She could hardly wait.

"All I wanted was to go somewhere exciting and do something worthwhile," she said to Emma.

"You didn't have to go quite so far away. I'm going to Southampton," said her friend. "That's far enough, and easy to get home."

"I don't want to get home easily," said Heather. "I just want to get away and be myself."

"You are funny," said Emma. "I don't see why you can't be yourself here."

"I can't explain. It's just something I need to do."

Katie understood. She had gone through a similar stage when she left home to work in the residential care sector. Yet her family situation had been uncomfortable, unhappy even, whereas Heather had been brought up in a secure and happy home. Was there something in their genes that made them want to wander and explore?

James had been a traveller, and so were her grandparents on her father's side. She'd never felt the need to move away from the area where she was born but Heather was different. Katie just hoped she would come back once her training was over.

When she'd asked Heather what Debbie was doing her daughter had laughed.

"Last I heard she was in London, auditioning for some talent show. I don't know and I don't care."

Katie wasn't sorry that friendship had run its course.

Bernard crouched in the trees surrounding the car park. For four nights he had kept up the vigil but nothing had happened, no-one had come. He was beginning to think he was wasting his time and that Katie was right.

He suddenly spotted a shadow by the side door of the centre, and a light shone out for a second. Someone had opened the door, from the outside. Could anyone besides Mr Dunn and Geoff have a key?

He considered the rest of the staff, the two youngsters; Karen, who did the displays, the lady who worked part time in the pet department, and old Stan, who must be over retirement age, but who had been promised a position when the garden centre near his home was closed. He was the indoor plant expert and had been the general mentor until it became apparent how much more up to date Bernard's training was.

The figure emerged from the side door carrying a large object. It seemed heavy, a tall bird bath, perhaps.

Bernard had been so engrossed with watching the door he hadn't noticed a large, dark car sliding into the wide entrance of the car park. It was not showing any lights and the driver got out and helped put the object into the boot.

Bernard huddled behind a tree and rang 999. "Police, please," he said. "There's a robbery at the garden centre."

"Who are you?"

"Bernard Longman. I work there."

"And your address is?"

"10 The Meadows, but I'm at Smallbridge Garden Centre, Stable Lane. They are stealing stuff. You must come quick."

"Can you describe what is happening, Mr Longman?"

"Two men are putting things into a car. It's a dark car. All the lights are off, but I don't think they'll be here much longer."

"Can you see the number plate?"

"No. It's sideways on to me. They're going!"

"Try to see which way it goes. We'll send the nearest patrol car."

Bernard rang off. Whoever they sent it would be too late.

He wandered over to the opening in the trees. Had he seen a flash of light as the car exited? If so he thought it had turned left, towards Smallbridge Lane, but then it could have gone either way. He shivered. How long would it take for the police to get there?

The police car arrived about ten minutes later and when they found Bernard was not a key holder they rang the manager. Once he had joined them they all went inside to see what was missing.

"The big bird bath, two smaller ones and a statue," said Mr Dunn as they surveyed the remains of the display.

"And a heron," said Bernard.

"If we could go somewhere and get a statement?" suggested the policeman.

"I'll take a look at the door," said his companion. "Did

you say it must have been opened with a key?"

"But I thought there were only four sets of keys," said the manager, "and I've put two away."

"We'll need to interview all the staff tomorrow as soon as they come in. Now, Mr Longman, could you go through exactly what you saw?"

Bernard told them the events of the night. He watched Mr Dunn frown as he repeated his opinion that the intruder had a key.

"There's no sign of a forced entry," said the second policeman.

"Then there's a key I didn't know about," muttered the manager. "Just wait until I find who has it. How could someone who works here think they could get away with stealing stuff?"

"We don't want to spook the perpetrator," said the policeman. "If there's nothing else missing we'll leave it for tonight and come back tomorrow. Good night, gentlemen."

Next morning all the staff arrived as usual except Stan as it was his day off.

Satisfied with the interviews the police asked for Stan's address. "We'll just pop over and see him," one of them said. "You never know, we could get lucky. Meanwhile, do you think you could draw the car for us, Bernard? It might give us a clue as to the make."

"Sure. I can do that," said Bernard, pleased that he could do something else to help. He began to sketch the shape of the car he had seen in the night.

"What's that lump on the roof?" asked the manager, looking over his shoulder, "a roof rack?"

"No. I don't know. I just remember it wasn't a smooth roof."

"You know what? It could be a taxi. Stan doesn't drive. He always comes to work by taxi. I bet he sticks to the same firm."

"Should we tell the police?"

"Yes. The more I think about it, the more I think it must have been him. He even could have had a key to your locker; they were brought over from the old site."

It was the clue the police had needed.

Once they started asking Stan about taxis he insisted it was the driver who had forced him to steal the ornaments.

"He said he never saw a penny," the police told Bernard and the manager. " He said it was all the taxi driver's idea. Now we have to see if we can find any evidence against him."

"You know who it is?"

"Oh yes. He always booked the same driver. We've got a warrant to search his premises. We're on our way there now."

"Does Debbie's Dad drive a taxi?" Bernard asked Katie that evening.

"Yes, why?"

"The police think a taxi driver helped steal those things from the garden centre."

"Oh, surely it can't be him?"

"They didn't say a name."

"Bernard, there's loads of taxi drivers in town."

"I know. I hope it wasn't him."

So do I, thought Katie.

Katie had made up her mind. Now that Heather was at college and Robbie was always at the farm she was going to learn to do something new. She was going to join the St John Ambulance Service.

She enquired at the centre and they were overjoyed with her experience. "You need to update your first aid and spend time with our operators," they said. "The specialist courses can be fitted in over the winter and you should be able to join a team next year. Meanwhile, let us know when you're available and you can sit in on as many calls as you can."

"Just wait until I'm fully qualified," she boasted to Tania at the gym. "I'll be at all the Summer Fairs and Sports Events, perhaps even the Races. It's given me something to look forward to."

"I couldn't do that," said Tania. "The sight of blood makes me sick. By the way, did you hear about Al?"

"No – what?" Katie's heart was thumping.

"He's been arrested. He had an allotment with a garage and it was full of stolen stuff. Some was from a garden centre."

"They did find some things missing a while back."

"Well – there you are then. What a Charlie!"

Why? thought Katie. Why did Al have to pick Smallbridge Garden Centre to rob?

Had Stan been bribed to incriminate her husband? If so, it hadn't worked. Would they imprison Al?

She wished, fervently, that he'd not come back into her life. He seemed to bring nothing but trouble.

It was too late in the season for Bernard to start outdoor bowls. He still felt as if the burglary had, in some way, been his fault, and no longer felt he wanted to socialise in case people asked him about it.

He would go to the Open Day they held when the weather got warmer. Meanwhile he had been given back the keys to the garden centre and was, once again, in charge of opening up every day.

Stan had been dismissed and Karen had been promoted to assistant manager. They had appointed a new assistant called Stacey who also gave flower arranging lessons. She rejuvenated the displays and seemed to have the same effect on all who met her. Work once again became a pleasure. Bernard was content.

Heather came home for Christmas, moaning about not being able to fit in enough driving lessons with the work she was expected to do.

"Wait until the summer and do them then," advised Katie.

"I will. I just want a rest. I'm going down to see Emma. Don't make tea for me."

Once on the open road she pedalled furiously to keep warm. The wind whistled in her ears and she wished she'd worn a hat – or a helmet. She'd arranged to meet Emma in the coffee bar in the old church.

She chained her bike to a nearby post and went inside. Emma was already sitting at a table, reading.

"Hi, Em. What you having?"

"Cappuccino, please, Heather, thanks."

Heather brought the drinks to the table and sat down.

"It's great to see you. You've changed your hair?"

"D'you like it? Mum says I look like a beetroot."

"Mums just don't get it, do they? Now, what's been going on while I was away?"

"You know about the garden centre?"

"Of course. Stan got fired. What happened to Debbie's Dad?"

"He got away with a big fine. He couldn't get the sack – he owns the firm – but he's lost a lot of customers. They didn't put him in prison because it was a first offence."

"The first time he was caught, you mean."

"I don't know. I think that family has problems."

"What's Debbie doing now?"

"She's working at a holiday camp – but that's seasonal, and Harry's not got a job."

"I suppose we're lucky."

"Yes. Tell me about your course. Have you met anyone special?"

"I haven't had time. I thought college would be all parties and late nights but they work us so hard we're too tired to go out most evenings. What about you?"

"I did meet someone I like – but when he came on to me I freaked out. All I could think of was Jack, and how he'd let me down."

"Give it time. Gee, it's great to be back. Let's go on the pier and pretend we're tourists."

She'd forgotten what a good place to relax in her home town was. She'd put aside all thoughts of skeletons and muscles for a while and just let herself float with the tide.

Robbie had named his puppy Shep.

The farmer had advised him to try it with basic obedience training first, before seeing if he could work with sheep, and Robbie had taken him everywhere with him to make sure he wasn't afraid of ordinary sights and sounds.

He'd even taken Shep to the last home athletics meeting of the season but Debbie wasn't there and he found he no longer really cared.

The girls he knew of his own age came over to make a fuss of the puppy and he realised there were more advantages to having a dog than he'd expected.

The puppy behaved superbly and he was certain that, together, they would make a great team. It was all he wanted to do.

Heather spent Easter with her grandmother in Wales.

Rose tried to make it enjoyable for her but there were no people of her own age, and although she liked to see her Nan happy, she wished she'd been able to go abroad like her room mate.

Going up the mountain in a little train and visiting the Italianate Village were no compensation for missing genuine foreign adventures.

Before she returned to college Rose let her choose a piece of jewellery for herself and she had her ears pierced so that she could wear a pair of gold studs.

The months flew by and Heather was absorbed by her studies.

At the end of the summer term she was satisfied that she had chosen the right course and was looking forward to coming home and learning to drive.

Pat's car had been waiting for her where her father had arranged to keep it, parked in the garden centre car park.

The old camping site now a fully functioning children's playground with climbing frames, tunnels and slides and a little pottery area in Chantelle's old shop where people could make their own mugs or plates.

It was not only the surroundings that had changed. Her family seemed rejuvenated.

Her brother's pets had all gone and he only came home to eat and sleep.

Her mother had joined the St John Ambulance and her kitchen diary was marked with the events she had to attend over the summer, and her father surprised her most of all.

He had been accepted as a member of the village bowls team and was out most evenings, practising.

His first competition was the second weekend after she returned home. It was difficult to imagine her father in a competition – and even harder to find he had the skill to be in the winning team.

"Dad – That was so cool!" she said afterwards, feeling slightly uncomfortable among the group of older men and their wives.

"I'm glad you were there," replied Bernard. "It was nice knowing you were watching."

"I never knew you could do that."

"Nor did I. I had a good teacher. Norman, the skip, was very patient with me."

A short, white haired man with a big moustache turned to greet them.

"Ah. Our new star has a delightful daughter," he said. "You must be Heather."

"Yes," She couldn't help blushing. "What has Dad been saying about me?"

"Only good things, my dear. Come and meet the wife. She'll tell you what it's like to have a bowler in the family. Well done, Young Bernard."

Young Bernard? Her father was over 50, but then, looking around her, Heather realised he was one of the youngest men there.

She watched as her father accepted the congratulations of the team. She felt like an outsider, the memories of when she was the one winner in the family flooding back.

She had lost that – the joy of instant success. She looked at her father's face – a mixture of pride and embarrassment. She knew he would soon want to get away.

Praise did not feed and nurture him as it had done her. He was surprised by success – she needed it to grow. Still, she was happy to have watched him. It would have been a pity if no-one from the family had been there to witness his first match.

Katie had arranged driving lessons twice a week for Heather during the holidays but by the time she was due to go back to college the instructor said she doubted Heather was ready. "I suggest you take the theory test now and do the practical when we're sure you'll pass," she advised.

It wasn't what Heather wanted, but she started her second year with at least one achievement. The theory test had been no problem, but she returned north still without a car.

Heather was in the hospital on the day the town hosted the charity fun run, a half marathon that many of the students were competing in.

She was miserable.

She sat in the staff restaurant, huddled over a cup of coffee and a Belgian bun, wishing she could join them.

There was a cheer from outside as the first few runners went past.

A shadow blocked out the light and a voice said, "Are you all right? Can I help?"

She looked up to see a tall man with light brown hair, slightly greying at the temples, hovering on the other side of the table. His blue eyes momentarily mesmerised her and she could not speak.

"May I sit down?" he said. "Perhaps you could tell me what's wrong?"

He put down what looked like a glass of milk shake and sat in the chair opposite.

Heather stifled a giggle. What was a man like him doing with a milk shake?

"That's better," he said. "My name's Neal – but you don't have to."

Heather laughed again at the weak joke. "I'm being stupid," she said at last. "If I'd been fit I'd be out there, running, but I had an accident and now I have to be careful."

"And why are you here?"

"I'm on a Physiotherapy course. This is all part of our training."

"I see, but let me look at your hands? Yes, I think you'll make an excellent physiotherapist."

Without realising what she was doing Heather had laid her hands flat on the table in front of her and Neal had taken hold of one and was gently massaging her fingers. She didn't dare pull away but it seemed a strangely intimate gesture.

Her face must have shown her alarm because her companion smiled and let go of her hand, saying, "Don't mind me, I'm a doctor."

"Oh, I'm sorry." Heather pulled her hands away as if she had been burnt. They had all taken note that they were forbidden to fraternise with the medical staff.

"We aren't inflammable," he said. "Some of us would like someone different to talk to."

"Where do you work?" asked Heather, unsure whether she wanted to know because she wanted to avoid him, or because she wanted to see him again.

"Men's orthopaedic – so we might bump into each other again." His smile was infectious. "I can test your knowledge," he teased.

"There's not much I don't know about broken bones," she said, bitterly.

"Ah, but I know more about mended ones," he joked – his voice sounding like a challenge.

No-one had seemed so relaxed in her company for months, especially not a man. She watched him drink his milk and run his tongue over his top lip to remove any excess.

He smiled again and she realised she had been staring at him. She blushed and looked down at her snack. It looked very unappetising now.

"Would you like another coffee?" he asked. "That must be cold by now."

"No, thank you." She pushed back her chair. "I'd better be going."

"Thanks for the chat," he said, "I'm sure we'll meet again."

Heather fumbled for her bag. She had to get away. Just being near him was making her jumpy.

She hurried out of the restaurant, leaving her half-eaten bun, not really sure where she was going, with "we'll meet again," ringing in her ears.

There was only one place where she could indulge her competitive spirit – the swimming pool, and she was determined to get into the University team. On days when the pool was not booked for racing some lanes were roped off for serious swimmers but the rest of the pool was open for leisure use. It was on one of these days that she met Neal again. They both came out of the changing rooms at the same time.

"Hallo there, mystery lady," he said, "You never told me your name."

"Heather," she said, shyly.

"Well, Heather. How's your swimming?"

"Quite good." She liked the challenge in his voice.

"How about a race?"

"Two lengths?"

"Fine."

He followed her to the part of the pool that had been divided into lanes and they waited until two were clear.

"Ready, steady, go," he chanted, and then seemed to wait a second before he set off.

Heather didn't want any favours – she knew she could beat any casual swimmer.

She kept up with him in a lazy crawl and then, just before the finish, kicked hard and reached the end before him. He was breathing heavily as they clung to the side.

"That was great," he said. "I haven't done that for months."

"You weren't letting me win, were you?" Heather asked.

"Of course not," but his face was exultant. She wasn't sure she could believe him.

"I'm going back where I belong," he said. "I clearly need more practice."

She couldn't think of a reply and watched while he

pulled himself out of the water and returned to the other side of the pool.

He's got a nice body, she thought. I wonder how old he is?

Swimming lengths seemed less enticing once Neal had gone, but she completed her usual routine and then went to get changed.

She looked for Neal when she was showered and dressed but there was no sign of him. She didn't usually stay for a drink but she would, just this once. She bought a hot chocolate from the machine and sat near the window.

There seemed something inevitable about the hand that rested on her shoulder and the hot chocolate that joined hers on the table.

"Hallo, again," he said, once more sitting opposite her. "I watched you. You can really go, can't you?"

"It's the only sport I can do, now," she said.

"What did you used to do?"

"Running, then hurdles. It was a fall over hurdles that finished me."

"So – did that make you choose physiotherapy?"

"I suppose so. I think I'd always wanted to do something like that but not known about it. Having it done to me showed me how valuable it was."

"You're right. Not enough people know what's involved. When do you qualify?"

"This is my second year." She was sure he was calculating her age. She took a sip of her drink. It was too hot.

"It must take ages to dry that long hair," he remarked.

"It's worse having to pin it up to go on the wards. It used to be shorter. I might do it again. It's better for racing."

"It suits you down."

The tone of his voice made Heather look at him. Was he coming on to her? she wondered. He seemed, somehow, to have become strangely intimate on the strength of two meetings. If that was so – what happened next?

"Where are you living?" he was asking – and she told him how she'd moved out of the college and found a house with three other girls. "We haven't been together long enough to work out who does what so it's a bit chaotic at the moment and we're all buying our own food. We've had to have a roster for the bathroom and there's not enough storage space, but I'm sure it'll settle down."

"I'm sure girls cope better. When I was at college we always ate out, even breakfast, when we had time for it – none of us were good cooks. Have you tried any of the local restaurants?"

He is coming on to me, she thought. He's going to ask me out. "Mainly the take-aways. It's cheaper to eat in college."

"Of course. Students are perpetually poverty stricken." He took a drink. "Well, next time I'll treat you to your chocolate."

He rose, put his cup in the bin and gave a nod. "Bye, Heather."

"Bye, Neal." Why did she feel so disappointed? He was way too old for her – probably mid thirties – yet he was so easy to talk to. He was going to be difficult to get out of her head.

14

It wasn't long before they met again.

This time Neal was giving a demonstration and, afterwards, if anyone had asked Heather what it was about she couldn't have told them.

It seemed natural, then, for her to go to him for advice, only to find that he was ready to see her more often.

It wasn't easy to find time to be together. Neal often worked at night and Heather's lecture programme was daunting.

She tried to keep up her enthusiasm for competitive swimming but among the students she always seemed to be the reserve and outside the racing clique. Her heart wasn't in it any more. None of the usual Uni activities gripped her. The debating society seemed full of eggheads and the play reading group immature show-offs.

Neal and Heather created their own routine. Once a week, when they were both off duty, they would go to the pool and then have a drink in the café.

It's entirely innocent, Heather told herself – but she was also aware that he was invading her thoughts much more than he should be.

She was reprimanded more than once for not attending in lectures.

Then, one Wednesday, Heather arrived at the pool and there was no sign of Neal.

She swam her usual lengths, watching out for him all

the time, but he did not appear.

When she returned to the changing room and turned on her phone there was a brief text. *Work.sorry.N.*

She realised, then, how much she looked forward to their encounters and felt real anger that his work had kept him from her. She wanted to hit out at something or someone. Instead she resolved to go out that evening and get drunk, or, as her friends would say, hammered.

Next day she was due back at the hospital but she felt so ill she couldn't get up.

Do people really enjoy this? she asked herself. She couldn't even remember much of the evening. She knew she'd stood on a table and sung and that she'd fallen down in the street but who she was with and where she went was a blur.

Her housemates had brought her home in the early hours and she'd slept until almost lunchtime, when she was violently sick and had a head that felt like rocks in a dustbin.

The next day her lecturer took her to one side and asked if she had any problems. "You were such a promising student last year," he said, "Is there anything wrong at home?"

"No. I haven't been feeling too well," she answered.

"If you're finding the work difficult I am here to help."

"It's not the work. It's just trying to organise my time."

"Well, it's good that you think like that. Try to get a balance between study and leisure. Come to see me if you can't cope."

"I will," she muttered, and fled. If she didn't sort herself out she was going to fail. She needed advice – and who better to give it than Chantelle. After all, she went off with a man much older than herself. She would know what to do about Neal.

"Chantelle. Can I come up for the weekend?" she asked over the phone.

"Of course, Heather. We'd love to see you. How's things?"

"I'll tell you when I get there. It's all a bit complicated."

When she got to the flat she couldn't stop herself. Not caring that James was listening she told Chantelle how she had met Neal – how she saw him every week – and how she couldn't imagine life without him.

"Oh, Heather, you have got it bad – but how do you know he's not married? An attractive man of his age is likely to be taken."

"We've talked and talked about our lives," Heather answered. "He was married but he's divorced. His wife left him and went to America."

"Have you seen his home?"

"Not yet. I know he's got a flat but we aren't supposed to date doctors. If anyone saw us we'd both be in trouble."

"So, realistically, you have to wait until you are qualified to get together?"

"Yes. I suppose so."

"Do you think he wants to?"

"I'm almost sure. He always compliments me and we like the same things. He's just so – perfect."

"Heather, no man is perfect." Chantelle looked over at Heather's grandfather. "What do you think, James?"

"I think she's way too young to think of settling down. I don't think her parents would approve and I hope she's got the sense not to do anything daft."

Heather was stunned. She'd always thought of her

grandfather as a rebel – and here he was talking like her mother. How dare he speak as if she wasn't there!

"Keep it casual, pet," said Chantelle, "and don't let it spoil your chances of a career. If he really loves you he'll wait a couple of years."

"Two years!" replied Heather. "It seems like a lifetime."

She returned to college determined to try to keep her work life and her social life separate – but when Neal phoned her to arrange their next swim she felt herself aching with anticipation.

The sight of him made her heart beat faster and she jumped out of the water to hug him.

After the swim he was waiting for her in the café. "Let's not drink here," he said. "I owe you more than that for letting you down last week. Let's go and have a meal."

"Where?"

"Not round here. I'll meet you in the car park. Do you like Chinese food?"

"I love it."

"There's a Chinese restaurant I know. I'll take you there. It'll be my treat. What do you say?"

"That would be wonderful. Thank you, Neal."

It isn't a date, she told herself. We're just going somewhere together for a meal. She wasn't even dressed up. She had on her grey track suit and trainers. Her hair was a mess and she'd only brought lipstick with her.

"Is it posh?" she asked, nervously, as they drove out of town.

"Not at all – and the lighting's so awful you can hardly see what you're eating, let alone the other diners."

He ordered wine with the meal and they had a

selection of dishes. He was telling her of his time at college and she almost confessed the night she had run riot – but she didn't. It would have made her sound too dependent on him.

His life as a child in Ireland was not so different from hers on the South Downs. His parents had been farmers. She told him about the time their new dog had chased the chickens and the flood that forced them to move.

"Are your parents still alive?" she asked.

"Unfortunately not. That's why I came to England. I still have a sister in Ireland."

"Do you want to go back?"

"I'm not sure. It depends on what I do next."

She told him, then, what her tutor had said about her work and he seemed very alarmed.

"Whatever you do, don't give up now," he said. "You'll make an excellent physiotherapist. If there's anything you aren't sure about I could coach you."

"Where would we go?"

"My place. I'll give you the address and let you know when I'm there – or would you prefer somewhere else?"

"I'd love to see your place," she replied – but there was a niggle of apprehension. Was he really offering to tutor her – or was he suggesting something else? If he was – did she mind?

That night she tossed and turned, wondering if she'd done the right thing. Finally she came to a decision. She'd take up his offer next term, when she came back after Christmas. That would give her time to get used to the idea.

It was a strange Christmas. Everyone seemed to be trying too hard to make it like it used to be, but they had all changed so much they didn't want to play the usual games or watch the usual programmes. Even the Christmas meal seemed too much – as if they had all changed their eating habits and couldn't revert to the mountains of meat, the Yorkshire puddings and the generous helpings of vegetables and roast potatoes.

Heather stared at her helping of Christmas pudding. "Can I leave it for later, Mum?" she asked.

Katie looked hurt but nodded assent. "I think we could all do with a walk," she said.

They donned raincoats and boots and set off up the hill. Even the countryside looks different, thought Heather, smaller, greyer and covered with litter.

The wind was cold at the top of the chalk rise and no-one seemed to have much to say to one another.

"I'll race you, Heather," said Robbie and then paused, looking at the furious expression on his sister's face.

"I'm sorry. I forgot."

"No-one should chase about on this uneven ground," said their mother. "Robbie, tell Heather what Shep can do."

"It's easier to show you," said Robbie. "Come down to the farm tomorrow."

"I might," replied his sister, "if I can't see Emma." But she didn't feel enthusiastic. She was missing Neal and wondering what he was doing for Christmas. He'd said he was going back to Ireland but he hadn't said where, or who he was seeing.

Heather was back at college for her birthday in February.

"*I'm cooking dinner tonight*" Neal texted and she had to tell her housemates she was going out.

"It's a good job we hadn't organised a party," moaned Vanessa. "If you're going to see your mystery man, be careful."

Heather grinned. She didn't know how much longer she could keep Neal a secret. One day someone would see her getting out of his car and put two and two together. She wished she could tell everyone about him.

At seven o'clock she stood on the doorstep of his flat.

It seemed like a special occasion. She had chosen to wear tight black trousers with a white shirt. Her newly washed hair was long and thick down her back and new earrings, a present from home, gleamed gold in her ears.

Although it was cold she hadn't wanted to wear boots and she had tottered to Neal's home in too-high heels and was longing to get inside and take them off.

Neal welcomed her with open arms and took her coat, hanging it on a hook in the hall.

His flat was not the minimalist den she had imagined. Instead it was a haven of brown and green, with a giant leather sofa and pale green walls. The closed curtains were brown and beige and the whole place felt comfortable and uncluttered.

"It's nearly ready," said Neal, "But first, this is for you."

He took a small box that had been lying by her place setting on the table and, kneeling in front of her, handed it to her to open.

She was so surprised at the gesture that she fumbled with the lid, but once she lifted it she let out a gasp of astonishment. Inside was a gold ring with a deep red stone in the centre, surrounded by tiny diamonds.

"I hope you like it," he said. "It made me think of you."

Heather took it out of the box and put it slowly onto her ring finger, hoping he would not correct her. It fitted perfectly.

"But we have to keep it secret?" she said. "I can't wear it all the time."

"You can when you're with me," he said, rising and pulling her with him.

He held her tightly in a strong embrace and gave her a lingering kiss.

"I love you, Heather," he said at last.

He'd never said it before. She felt weak at the knees. Why hadn't he waited until after the meal? Now she felt all churned up inside and not at all like eating. There was a creamy, mushroomy smell coming from the kitchen.

"What are you cooking?" she asked.

"Spaghetti carbonara. There's a red wine on the table or white in the fridge if you'd prefer."

"I'll try the red." She poured herself a glass. It had better not be too dry, she thought, but it wasn't. It was fruity and warming and there was a bowl of tiny cheese biscuits on the table so she helped herself to a handful and tried to calm down.

"What have you been doing today?" he asked conversationally as he brought in the food, and she began to relax as she told him.

Soon they were laughing and chatting as naturally as ever.

The dessert was tiramisu – her favourite, and afterwards she helped him load the dishwasher.

"I found some DVD's you might like to watch," he said. "Tell me if you've seen these."

She was curious to see what he had selected. There was an odd mix, from Gone with the Wind to modern ghost stories. "These are a bit romantic, aren't they?" she asked, archly.

"I felt romantic when I thought of you."

It seemed natural, then, to snuggle up together on the sofa and watch the movie.

"This is cosy," she muttered.

"It would be cosier in bed," he replied.

Her pulse raced. This was what she had feared, or expected. Had she secretly hoped that he would make love to her tonight?

She'd had a bath and washed her hair. Hadn't she really been preparing for this?

Wasn't it old fashioned to be a virgin at twenty, and hadn't he practically proposed to her?

"I love you, Heather," he said again. "It's been so hard to resist you all these months. Just come and lie down with me, please."

There was nothing Heather wanted to do more. "I'll just pop to the bathroom if you'll tell me where it is," she giggled.

"Certainly. I'll be waiting for you. I forgot you hadn't seen the rest of the place."

This is my last chance to get away, Heather thought, once she was alone. If I stop it now – that will probably be the end. She couldn't.

The months of meetings had reached their inevitable conclusion. She knew everything about the man she loved, except what it was like to be loved by him. She just hoped he would not be disappointed.

She left the bathroom and crossed the corridor to the bedroom.

Neal's lovemaking was as skilful and considerate as she had hoped it would be.

"Why don't you let me undress you," he said as she lay back, watching his face. His blue eyes looked tender and loving as he slowly removed her clothes.

"Are you ready for this?" he asked.

"Yes," she murmured, and then stopped thinking and let her body be swept away on a maelstrom of pleasure. When she became tense he paused and soothed her, eventually leaving her with such a feeling of fulfilment that she felt bound to him for ever.

She'd never expected her overwhelming reaction to be gratitude – but it was. She was so happy that her first experience had been with the man she was destined to marry.

"Can I tell my family about you?" she asked afterwards.

"Naturally – but not anyone here. You must get your degree before we reveal our plans."

Our plans – what a wonderful phrase, she thought. She could plan in her head, couldn't she? She could plan their wedding, plan their life as a team, even plan where they might live and work together. Life was going to be so exciting now she had someone to share it with. She looked over at Neal to thank him and was astounded to find him asleep. How could he sleep at such a momentous time?

Heather lay on her back, day dreaming for a while, and then began to feel uncomfortable. She gently slid out of the bed and went into the bathroom for a wash. She tried to dress without waking him but he stirred and opened his eyes.

"Can't you stay the night, beautiful?" he said, dreamily.

She felt such a fool. How could she have expected

him to run her back at that hour? "I didn't bring any…" she stuttered.

"Take it all off," he laughed, holding out his hand to her. "I'll keep you warm," and he did, although it took her a long time to fall asleep in his arms.

15

Knowing Neal loved her seemed to energise Heather. She attacked her studies with renewed vigour now she knew their future might depend on her success.

They continued to meet at the swimming pool until one day the event that she had dreaded occurred.

She came out of the toilet to hear two voices she knew. A couple of nurses from the hospital were getting changed to go in the pool.

She paddled swiftly through the foot bath and looked for Neal. He was in the pool already, doing lazy breaststroke while he waited for her.

She bent down by the water and beckoned to him. "We can't be seen together," she said. "There's two nurses in the changing room."

"Right. I'll stay here until they're in and then I'll get out and wait in the car. It was bound to happen one day."

"We need to find somewhere else to meet," he said, when she eventually joined him.

"Once I pass my test I can bring my car up here."

"Let's go out into the country and find a pub."

He sounded tired, she thought. He never spoke much about his work but she knew he was on duty for very long hours.

It was the end of Heather's second year. Her work had improved with her mood and she looked on course to get a good degree.

She had arranged for her fiancé to drive her home and meet the family. She'd called him, *my boyfriend* on the phone and hadn't made an issue of his age. She hoped and prayed that they would be as charmed by him as she was.

Katie didn't know what to do. Heather was bringing her new boyfriend home and it sounded serious. How was she going to sleep them?

Heather had a single bed in her room and the spare bed was in the computer room. If she'd been certain her daughter's friendship was platonic she would not have hesitated to put him in there – but she had the impression their relationship had passed that stage.

Still, she didn't intend to buy a double bed for her unmarried daughter.

She couldn't talk about it to Bernard. Instead, she asked Tania.

"You need to spell it out to Heather so she understands," said her friend. "Say you realise times have changed but in your house you would prefer it if they slept in their own beds."

"It sounds as if I am assuming they are lovers."

"Well, you are, aren't you?"

"She knows I wouldn't approve."

"Well then, you're half way there. Put it like this – please would she tell her friend that, as an example to Robbie, you would like them to sleep apart."

"I hadn't thought of that."

"Problem solved. Come on, get moving."

Neal had arranged to stay for the weekend and then go back to the hospital as his leave had been booked for Christmas when he was going to take Heather to Ireland.

Heather took a taxi to the railway station as usual, where he was waiting in the car park. "Get in, quick," he said. "I think I've seen someone who knows us."

He loaded her case into the boot and drove out.

There was something different about him.

Heather looked sideways at his profile and then had to stifle a giggle. "You've done something to your hair," she said.

"I've just had it cut."

"The grey's gone!"

"Well, there wasn't much there."

"Neal, have you dyed your hair to impress my parents?"

Neal slowed the car and brought it to a halt. "It's years since I did anything like this. I'm nervous, right? I love you very much and I don't want anything to spoil it. Allow me a little vanity, please."

She kissed him, then, amazed at his vulnerability.

"It'll be fine. I've told my Mum how I feel about you and you'll love my Dad. He's the most unpretentious man you could ever meet."

She wasn't worried about what the family would think of Neal – but she was concerned about what Neal would make of her father. Would he worry that any children they might have would be slow, like Bernard? It had crossed her mind but she had dismissed it as impossible. With parents like them, how could they produce a child that was below average? She settled back to enjoy the journey. It was a long way to Sussex.

Katie's first reaction when she saw Neal was, *I wish I had a doctor like that*. She could see why Heather adored him but what did he see in a temperamental madam like her daughter?

Oh, she was aware that Heather was dedicating her life to caring for others now – but Katie wasn't fooled – she knew that her daughter just wanted to prove she was better than all of them, cleverer and of more use to society. There were a hundred different ways Heather could compete with those around her and her career was only one of them. It seemed as though competitive swimming had taken a back seat now she was involved in a romance.

She had spotted the ring on Heather's finger. "I suppose you're going to tell us you're officially engaged," she said. "Doesn't anyone ask the father any more?"

"Don't be bitchy, Mum. Why do you think Neal came down here with me? He couldn't ask over the phone, could he?"

"Well, you tell him. I don't want any creeping about in the night – whatever you've been used to up there."

"OK. We get the message. Don't give him a hard time."

"Mrs Longman – delighted to meet you." Neal had unloaded the cases and was holding out his hand.

"For goodness sake call me Katie. Come in and have a drink. You must be parched."

Robbie had been given strict instructions to be at home for dinner with their guest and Katie was glad he was because Neal seemed fascinated by his work with the sheepdog. "Can I come and see him tomorrow?" he asked.

"Sure. Did you have sheep on your farm?"

"Yes – but I didn't have a dog of my own. I never really understood sheep. Perhaps I didn't study them enough."

"There's usually one ewe that's the boss and the others follow her," said Robbie.

"Sounds familiar," muttered Heather and her mother gave her a stern glare.

"Heather tells me you design coffee tables, Bernard," said Neal, turning to his host. "Have you any at home?"

"There's one in the conservatory," replied Bernard, "and two more not finished in the shed. Would you like to see them before it gets too dark?"

"That would be great. It was a lovely meal, Katie – or can I call you Kate?"

"I've been waiting for someone to do that for years," replied Katie. "I've told people but they just forget."

"Oh, he won't forget," said Heather. "He reminds me when I have to give in work at college."

"I can see you're good for her, Neal" said Katie, with a conspiratorial smile.

Neal just nodded, and followed Bernard into the garden.

"You like him, don't you, Mum?" said Heather as they moved into the kitchen.

"He seems nice – but how old is he?"

"A lot younger than you. He's wonderful, Mum. Just think of it – your daughter, married to a doctor!"

"Oh, yes – and when will that be?"

"Next summer, we hope. I told Neal I'd never been abroad and he said why didn't we choose somewhere really romantic."

"That sounds expensive."

"No it isn't. There's plenty of time to sort that out. It's

so exciting, Mum. I've never felt so happy."

"Your father says there's a nice little pub in the village," said Neal when they returned from the shed. "How about a walk?"

"What would he know? He never used to go to pubs," Heather retorted and then realised how immature she had sounded. Why did she have to revert to 'child' mode just because she was home? "At least, not unless it was to take Mum out to dinner," she added.

"You show Neal the village, darling," said Katie. "I expect you could do with stretching your legs after that long drive."

They hadn't got out of the Close before Heather was asking, "Well? What did he say?"

"Who?" Neal teased.

"My Dad. You did ask him, didn't you?"

"The subject did come up, yes."

"And what did he say?"

"He said what I expected him to say – that you were old enough to make up your own mind and if I loved you and could make you happy that was fine by him."

"Terrific! I'm so glad you've won them over. Oh, you darling, darling man!"

"Steady on. What will the neighbours think?"

She was jumping up and down, clinging to his arm. "I'd like to run and run and run," she declared, waving her arms around wildly in the air.

"Well don't run too far – I don't know which way we're going."

Once Neal had gone back Heather's old feeling of being left out returned.

Her father was either working or bowling, her mother was off to all sorts of events when she wasn't dealing with feet, and Robbie was away with the sheep on the farm.

All she had to look forward to was her driving test.

She rang Emma but there was no reply so she rode down to her house to see if she was there.

"I'm sorry, love," said Emma's mother when she arrived. "She's gone on holiday with a bunch of other girls. They're in Majorca."

"Everyone's doing something exciting except me," grumbled Heather. "When will she be back?"

"In a fortnight. I'm sure she'd love to see you then."

"I'm doing my driving test in three weeks. If I pass I can take her out somewhere."

"That'll be great, dear. She'll be pleased you called."

Heather had brought her costume so she made her way to the swimming pool but it was full of noisy children and she began to get a headache.

Miserable now, she pushed her bike along the prom, staring at the sea.

"Hi, Heather." Another bike appeared next to hers. It was Stephen.

"Hallo, Steve. Not working?"

"It's my lunch break. I'm at the photographer's in the High Street now. How's college?"

"Going well. One more year and I'll have my degree."

"Want to come for a sandwich?"

"Sure."

They sat outside the café at the old cinema and Heather found herself telling Stephen about Neal. "We're going to get married in Mauritius," she said, "and then find a general practice or even set up on our own, so that I can have a base at his surgery and we can offer traditional medicine and physiotherapy."

"Where would this be?" asked Stephen.

"I don't know. I'd like to stay up north but I think he's planning somewhere more affluent."

"You wouldn't consider down here?"

"I might, but I wouldn't push it. Brighton might be fun."

She tried to imagine herself and Neal as a married couple, walking together along the sea shore. A picture of a young child, running on the pebbles and throwing stones into the sea flashed into her mind. What would she want most for any child of theirs? Country air, no crime and a good school. But she didn't even know if Neal wanted children. It was something they would have to discuss. It was hard to think beyond the next few months. If she started dreaming about the future she lost sight of the present.

"Are you seeing anyone?" she queried.

"No-one special. I do go to the night club now and again. Why don't you come on Friday night?"

"I'd love it. I'm getting bored stiff at home."

"We meet in the pub on the front at 8.30. See you there. I must get back to the shop."

"See you." She gave him a wave as he rode away. Now she felt better.

Sitting back she listened to the seagulls. The sun shone on the water and the day seemed somehow brighter. She hadn't been out in a crowd for months. It was going to be a good holiday after all.

In fact, it turned out to be a great holiday. Not only did she catch up with her friends from her schooldays but she also passed her driving test.

First time! she e-mailed Chantelle. *I never expected to pass first time. I'll have so much more freedom. I'll be up to see you and show off.*

She sent a text to Neal; *Passed my test today. Driving up Tues.Luv.H.*

Neal rang back that evening. "Hallo, darling. Congratulations."

"Isn't it wonderful? I won't have to feel so wicked creeping out of your car any more."

"It will certainly help. Ring me as soon as you get back. I'm not working that night."

"I will. I love you, Neal."

"Me too. Give my best wishes to your family. Bye, love."

She hugged herself with delight. She couldn't have asked for more. Next year she would become Mrs Neal O'Connor. *Heather O'Connor*, she tried out for the umpteenth time. It sounded perfect.

Having a car made life very different for Heather but the main change was something she had not foreseen.

She had no money. At least - she had money, but it was all in savings and she was having to spend them on a daily basis. She was living beyond her means.

Her time with Neal had also changed. She no longer went to his flat. Instead, about once a month, they drove out of town, separately, and spent the weekend at a country hotel. It was like having lots of mini honeymoons and was enough to keep the romance alight.

Heather had broached the subject of children as soon as she had returned.

At first Neal seemed not to take the subject seriously. "We'll let nature take its course," he had said, glibly. But Heather had insisted on discussing it until finally he had succumbed.

"To be honest," he said, "at the moment I wouldn't want children, at least for the first two or three years. Once we are established, and if we could afford it, I could probably be persuaded – if you were keen."

"You aren't saying you never want any?"

"No. I think you'd make a great mother."

"That's OK, then. Decision deferred. You're brill."

"And you're sexy." He rolled over on top of her and kissed her nose. "Love me again," he said, and she did.

16

Rose was disappointed. Not only had she not met Heather's young man, she had been told that the wedding was to be held abroad and she was not invited.

Bernard and I are going to Mauritius with them for two weeks and then they are having a big reception here when we get back, wrote Katie. *He's a doctor. His name is Neal O'Connor and he's making Heather very happy.*

We are all getting passports at last. Robbie may need one to go skiing with the school. Having Neal in the family has made me feel more adventurous. There's a big wide world out there.

Now Heather's passed her test I'm sure she'll want to drive over to see you. They are going away together for Christmas but we'd love to see you if you can make it.

Love, Katie.

"I'm not going back there this year," Rose told Sarah. "It's the wrong time to be travelling. If they want to see me they can come here."

"I've never seen you angry before, Rose."

"I don't agree with people going off together before they are married," said Rose. "It's just not right."

"She's only doing what everyone else does nowadays."

"I don't want to think about it. He just better be good to her." Rose stomped down the shop and began rearranging tins on the shelf. She had been looking forward to seeing her granddaughter in a long white dress, walking up the aisle with a beautiful bouquet. Now all she'd see would be wedding photographs, and she'd have to go to England for the party.

She knew that not all marriages that begin in a church ended happily, her own for one, but to be left out of proceedings altogether! She felt hurt. She tried to feel happy for Heather but she couldn't help feeling she had been punished, somehow, for not staying in England.

Heather was apprehensive about Christmas. Neal wouldn't tell her where they were going, or if they were going to meet any of his family.

"Just be prepared to be cosseted," he said. "We're going to my favourite place in all the world."

It turned out to be Dublin. They stayed in a hotel near the centre and he made sure she experienced all the tourist delights, including the trip to the roof of the most famous brewery in Ireland.

"I can't drink all this," she giggled, holding the free pint of brown liquid.

"You drink what you can and I'll finish it."

Heather was amazed at the shops. She wanted to wander round the large stores on her own but Neal stayed by her side. He had selected a small hotel, smart but not luxurious, with delicious breakfast and varied dinners. It should have been magical, but for some reason she missed the traditional Christmas with her family. Christmas is for children, she told herself. One day we'll make our own traditions.

She started the term with a cold and kept away from Neal for a week until she was better.

She had to make up the work she had missed but was content to let him arrange the wedding trip, buying the tickets and booking the hotel for the four of them.

"We have to go for just over two weeks before the day," he told her. "Your mother and father will have to take three weeks off. Can they do that?"

"As long as they give plenty of notice," she answered.

"October looks like the best month," he said. "We should be sorted by then."

"It's a pity Robbie can't get time off school."

"There's still the reception to organise. Can your mother do that?"

"She's already planning it. I think they want to use the garden centre."

"What a brilliant idea. I'll give them the dates as soon as I've booked our flights."

Heather drove Robbie to Wales for Easter. She needed to convince her Nan that she was doing the right thing.

She knew Robbie would be in his element with the Evans family and she felt that having a car would help her to get away and explore.

Her grandmother seemed genuinely delighted to see her, but reluctant to hear about Neal.

"You'd love him if you met him, Nan," she pleaded.

"I'm sure I would, but let's just enjoy the time we have together and leave the future to take care of itself," she said, when Heather started to tell her about the wedding plans.

It was the perfect place to forget in, she thought. I'll allow myself a tiny breathing space. The intensity of the last few months seemed to fade away.

She no longer cared that there was no-one her age to spend time with. In fact, she enjoyed being by herself – there had been so few days when she could spend time as she wished.

Slowly the beauty and peace of the landscape began to work their magic on her and she felt herself relaxing as she sat at the top of the cliff with her knees up to her chin. 'Harmony' she thought. That's what this place makes me think of. Stephen would love it.

All too soon she was back at work, making the final effort to complete her course.

By the time she arrived home in the summer, plans for the reception were in full swing. Without really discussing it the cost of the wedding had been divided – the trip to be paid for by Neal and the reception by Heather's parents.

The garden centre was doing the catering, Stacey was doing the flowers and a young local band had been booked on the understanding that they could play anything from the sixties to the present day.

The guest list was proving contentious. Heather had given her mother a list of her friends from the local college and the athletics club and then had watched, astounded, as Katie added her own friends and their children.

"Tania and Duane will bring Oliver, you know him, and Emma's mum and brother should come. David and Susan will bring Patrick, if he's available. He and his wife have a big house in London. Lucy is still living at home. She's a hairdresser, you know, perhaps she'll do your hair."

"I don't want it done," said Heather. "I just want it long and loose. I'm having it up for the wedding."

"Who's coming from Neal's side?"

"His sister from Ireland and two colleagues from the hospital, one with his wife. He said if we write their invitations he'll take them. They're organising his stag night."

"We could have sent his sister's. Still, perhaps he wants to add something."

"He hasn't told me much about her. I hope she approves of me."

Heather looked at her mother for reassurance but Katie didn't seem to notice.

"Well, I still have to write to Lisa but I don't think they'll be able to make it. It depends when Ryan is home. Will your friend Steve take photo's?"

"Of course."

"Your father is inviting the garden centre staff – at least, those that aren't working."

"He's not inviting the bowlers, is he?"

"No. He says they don't really know you."

"Good, and Robbie?"

"I don't know. The people at the farm, I suppose, and Naz. He doesn't really talk about anyone else."

"He doesn't talk about anyone any more – just Shep, Shep, Shep."

"Well, they've been really good to him. They said he could stay there while we were away. I didn't want him to have to cope on his own."

"Emma's coming with me to choose clothes," said Heather. "Something light and floaty for Mauritius and colourful and trendy for back here."

"Where are you going for all that?"

"Brighton, of course. It's the nearest thing to London," and she flounced out.

Katie was driving the ambulance back from a demonstration. It was pouring with rain and she was slowing to round a bend when there was an ominous crashing sound from in front of them.

As they turned the corner they saw a sight of utter devastation. A white van had come to a halt, half across the pavement. A car was buried in its rear – the front end crumpled and one wheel spinning across the road.

Katie pulled in behind it and her companion jumped out to put warning cones across the road.

One man, presumably the van driver, was walking dizzily along the pavement, holding onto the wall. As she reached him he collapsed, sliding down with his back against the brickwork.

Katie turned to look for the driver of the car. It wasn't a car, it was a taxi – Al's taxi- and the air bag inside had done its job.

Al was out cold – but still alive. She ran to the door and opened it, then paused. She didn't want to leave him in the car, but she didn't dare move him on her own.

Her companion was calling for aid and they could hear a siren in the distance.

Al was carefully brought out of the wrecked car and the two casualties were soon on their way to hospital.

Katie wasn't sure if Al had seen her or not – but he had muttered, "Thank you," as he was lifted into the vehicle.

When Heather's results came she was overjoyed to find she'd managed a 2.1. She was a Bachelor of Science.

All the immediate family attended the graduation ceremony.

Her mother drove them up to the university and they

stayed for a couple of nights in a small hotel.

Best of all, Chantelle came for the day to witness Heather's success and take lots of photographs.

"James will be over the moon," she said, "and he's sent a message for Robbie. He's told me the address of his nephew's farm in Yorkshire. He says they have plenty of sheep."

"Thank him very much," said Katie, "But Robbie's already had an offer of a job from the family in Wales."

The only person who did not attend was Neal. After all the months of keeping their liaison secret he said he wouldn't spoil it by joining them, possibly causing a load of gossip.

In a way, Heather was glad, because she'd already told one of her house mates that she was engaged and promised to let her know who it was before the wedding.

"You'll all be getting invitations to the reception," she said, "So I need your home addresses."

"It's a doctor, isn't it?" said Vanessa. "We've been taking bets on which one."

"I'll tell you later. We're going for a curry now. I'll ring you."

She knew once she had told one of them the news would spread like wildfire and hoped that Neal wouldn't mind. After all, she was no longer a student. In three months she would be Mrs Neal O'Connor, the physiotherapist.

Katie wore her uniform to the hospital. If she saw any of Al's family it would be an official visit, just to check up on a casualty.

He was sitting up in bed, looking unhappy. His hair

is receding, she thought. How could I ever have thought him handsome?

Then he spotted her and a wide grin spread across her face. "My guardian angel!" he said. "Have you come to see me?"

"Yes, you old reprobate. I've come to see how you are and ask you what on earth you were doing, stealing stuff from the garden centre."

"It was a stupid idea. I thought if I could get your husband in trouble I'd have a chance with you. Stan was willing, the old fool. Trust him to balls it up!"

"Stan felt Bernard had taken his job. But now you've got a criminal record."

"People will forget. Carol still has a job. We'll manage. They say I'll be out in a week."

"You never did have a chance with me, you know. I suppose it was you that left the flowers and the photo?"

"I hoped we could get back to how we were."

"Not by making me run out of petrol."

"I know. That was really idiotic. But it worked, didn't it? I wanted you to remember me."

"It was a long time ago, Al. We're different people now."

"Thanks for everything, Katie. Without you I might not be alive."

"That was just luck."

"Maybe, but I was glad it was you. It's given me a chance to say sorry."

"Just get better, and no more following me around," she scolded.

"I wouldn't dare. You look too scary in that uniform."

She couldn't help smiling. He hadn't really changed.

17

Heather was in limbo. The wedding was almost organised but she had no idea of what she was going to do afterwards.

She hadn't seen Neal for weeks and even his e-mails had got briefer.

"He's applying all over the place for positions for us," she told Emma over the phone. "It's so annoying not knowing where we're going to live when we are married."

"Would it matter if it was his flat?" asked Emma.

"I suppose not. I'm not sure what his friends would think. They're all older than me. I wanted us to move somewhere new."

"There's a letter for you on the hall table," called her mother.

"I'm just coming." She said goodbye to her friend and hurtled down the stairs.

"It's from Neal," she cried. "I wonder if he's got a new job."

She ran back upstairs with the letter and sat, crossed legged, on the bed. She wanted to hug the news to herself before she told anyone else. She put her forefinger under the flap and ran it along, ripping the paper unevenly in her eagerness to read the contents.

It was a fat letter. A thick envelope dropped to the floor and a thin sheet of paper rested on her hand. She unfolded the letter.

Dear Heather,

I am sending you the tickets for Mauritius. Everything is paid for and as it is half term I hope Robbie can go with you. I've put his name as the fourth one anyway.

You will realise that it is because I cannot come with you.

I am sorry. Thinking we could get married was a mistake.

I do still love you, but I am not free. My wife in America would not divorce me.

In fact, I am going over there to see if we can make a go of it.

It was my fault she left, and if I hadn't met you I might have gone earlier.

You have made the last year so special and I am sorry to hurt you like this – but I know you are resilient and you have a wonderful family to support you.

Please do take the holiday and Best Wishes for the future,
Neal.

Heather could feel her heart beating in her throat. Her chest felt tight and her skin clammy.

She read the letter a second time - to make sure she'd understood. Then she picked up the package from the floor. It was a small wallet, full of travel tickets, a booklet about Mauritius and even some Mauritian currency.

Through tears she studied the tickets. Sure enough, they were made out to her, her mother and father and Robbie. How long had he been planning this? she wondered. Had he ever intended to marry her?

She let out an agonised scream, "Noooo," and, throwing the papers across the room, buried her head in the pillow.

Her mother came rushing into the room. Heather's shoulders were heaving.

"Look!" she squealed. "Look at that letter!"

Katie picked the paper from the floor and did as she was asked. By the time she had finished reading Heather was sitting up, her back against the headboard, her face red with fury.

"How could he! Does he really think we'd go without him? What would people think?"

"Oh, Heather. You poor darling." Her mother folded her in her arms.

"What can I do, Mum? I feel such a fool."

"No you're not. You just fell for the wrong man, that's all. It happens all the time. You have a good cry. I'll see to everything else."

She picked up the tickets and, closing the door gently behind her, went downstairs.

The first person Katie rang was her mother. "The wedding's off, Mum," she said. "Neal is still married. He's gone to America."

"Thank goodness for that," responded Rose. "I thought he was too good to be true. She's not pregnant is she?"

"No. Of course not. They knew what they were doing."

"Well, he did, anyway. How's she taken it?"

"Pretty badly so far – but if I know my daughter she'll soon bounce back. He's sent the travel tickets."

"You aren't going, are you?"

"It's up to Heather – but I think we ought to. It would be something we could never afford to do ourselves. It's all paid for."

"What about the reception?"

"I'll cancel that. Besides, once we get back Heather will be looking for a job."

231

"Well, she's welcome here anytime. Give her my love."

"I will, Mum, thanks."

When Bernard and Robbie came in Katie told them the news.

Bernard immediately went upstairs and knocked on his daughter's door.

"Who is it?"

"Dad. Can I come in?"

"I suppose. I'm not coming down."

He opened the door and stepped inside.

"I don't want any tea," Heather began. "I don't want anything."

Bernard sat at the end of the bed. "We love you," he said simply.

"I know, but it hurts. I thought I was going to be with him for ever. He never seemed like a cheat. He never seemed like he was lying. How could I get it so wrong?"

Bernard let her rage on, shaking her head from side to side. He could hear the incredulity in her voice, the dismay that love had blinded her to her fiancé's faults, and the anger that she had been so easily deceived.

"He's made me look an idiot," she finished. "I can't face anyone."

"Your mother says she'll bring you a cup of tea when you're ready. Would you like a jam tart?"

Heather stared at him through her tears and then burst out laughing. "Oh. Dad – you don't know how funny that sounds in the circumstances. Poor Heather, she's just been jilted – lets give her a jam tart!"

Bernard was confused – but he was glad he'd made

her smile. "I'll see you later," he said and backed out of the room.

Three days later Katie called a family conference.

Heather had come down for breakfast the next day but had refused to go out. She joined them for meals and then retreated into her bedroom.

Katie guessed she was e-mailing Chantelle and Emma but her daughter spoke little. She wore her scruffiest clothes and scraped her hair back into a ponytail. It was as if she was in mourning.

She is, thought Katie. She's mourning for the life she might have had.

They all sat round the kitchen table and Katie brought out the tickets for Mauritius. "Now, Heather," she began. "There's five thousand pounds in my hand, but if we give them back we'll only get a fraction of that because it's so near. Is it possible that we could go as a family holiday or would it be too painful for you?"

"I've been thinking about that," replied her daughter. "I think we should go. In a way it would serve him right if we had a fabulous time that he'd paid for. No-one there will know us, or care that the wedding is off. At least I'd have got something out of this relationship."

"Good. Then all we have to do is get permission for Robbie to come out of school. I know it's exam year but I don't think they'll object."

"They don't expect me to pass any exams anyway," said Robbie. "I'm leaving as soon as I can."

"Well, Ned, do you agree?"

"With going on holiday? Yes. It's a long way on an aeroplane, isn't it?"

"Yes, Dad," Heather joined in, "But you'll love it when

you get there. You can go snorkelling."

"That's settled then," said her mother. "Heather, it's about time you came back to the real world. Decide where you want to work and get applying."

"I've been looking on the web. I think I've made up my mind. I'll let you know when I'm sure."

I knew she'd be OK, thought Katie. I wonder where she's applying to?

Hi Chantelle,

Mauritius was wonderful. The flight was uncomfortable but the hotel was like a palace. It was right on the sea shore with palm trees and beautiful gardens and exotic birds.

The pool was enormous and no-one seemed to use it except us. The food was fabulous and there was live music every night. Granddad would have loved it.

Robbie fell in love with the giant tortoises – they had them at all stages of their lives. They breed them for other islands.

Mum and Dad liked the tea plantations and brought back loads of peculiar fruit teas.

I've been accepted at a hospital in the Midlands. I start after Christmas. I really missed being up north. This will be perfectly placed between you, Nan and here.

I can't wait to find somewhere to live and get started.

My love to you both, Heather.

"Mum, I want to ask you something really odd."

"Oh, yes. What?"

"Do you think Dad would mind if I changed my name?"

"What on earth do you mean?"

"Well, when I start out as a physiotherapist I would like to be known as Heather Long – not Heather Longman. It looks more businesslike."

"You mean, just as a work name, not permanently?"

"Yes, like an actress or a writer."

"What about the banks and the NHS?"

"I'd have to enquire. I just want to know what Dad would say. I wouldn't want to upset him."

"I don't think he'd be upset. I'll ask him. You are a funny one."

Bernard listened while Katie told him what his daughter had requested. "She wants to call herself Heather Long," she said. "Would you mind?"

"Not really. She was going to change her name when she got married, wasn't she? If it makes her feel good – let her do it."

Why didn't she talk to me? he thought. People always go to Katie first. Only Robbie tells me things he doesn't tell other people. He would have come straight to me, but he would never think of changing his name.

Once he'd begun to think about his son his mood changed. He had been trying to come to terms with the way his family was dividing – its members scattering across the country. The change he found hardest to accept was Robbie's latest plan – to move to Wales. There were plenty of sheep in England, weren't there?

He didn't want his son to leave. He wanted to watch him grow into a man and share his obvious enjoyment of life. Seeing Robbie happy made Bernard happy. If only he and Katie were left he wasn't sure life would be as pleasant.

It made him feel old just to think of it. He wasn't ready for retirement. The holiday in Mauritius had been exhausting but it had given him a taste for new experiences.

Without Heather and Robbie all his activities would be among older folk. He didn't want that. What could he do about it?

He would ring Zak for suggestions.

Zak was sorry about Heather's abandonment but thrilled to hear of her success.

"I'm glad you called," he said. "I'm coming down your way. The group that organises holidays for the disabled have a trip to your town. Each of us has an assistant with us, like you were for me at college – and we have a week in a specially adapted hotel. I know it's not the summer but it will be a change."

"Zak – you're terrific. Could I join this group?"

"You mean as a helper? Well, not straight away. You'd have to find your local section and see if they needed anyone. With your experience they'd snap you up. I'll contact you when I get there. The seaside in December – brrr!"

Zak rang off and Bernard went to tell Katie about his impending visit. He wouldn't mention his other plans until he was sure they could use him.

Katie had plans of her own. With Heather and Robbie both moving away she was considering letting one of the rooms.

She would be able to choose when they had visitors, and it would bring in extra income. She had resented the time her mother had spent on her guests when she ran the B and B at Lane's End but, on reflection, now recognised that it could be interesting to have new people popping in and out of their lives.

She would need to put twin beds in Robbie's room. Heather's was smaller and she would prefer to rent to couples rather than single people.

If Robbie and Heather wanted to come home at the same time Robbie could sleep in the spare room, with the computer. She would keep Heather's room vacant but redecorate it so it wasn't so girly.

Robbie wasn't moving completely until after the New Year. She would have to try to make Christmas extra special for all of them.

Rose had been busy supervising the preparations for her grandson's arrival.

Rhys's brother already lived over the stables but there was room to convert two more loft spaces to accommodate Robbie. He would have to share a bathroom and kitchen but would have a bedroom and living room of his own.

"There is an empty cottage but we wouldn't give that to a single shepherd," Rhys explained. "He's bringing his own dog, isn't he?"

"Yes. Shep. The only thing is, he's too young to drive. I'm staying over the New Year and then Katie is bringing us both back together."

"We'll miss you, Rose. Have a good holiday."

"I will." She was glad she was going to see all of them together, especially after Heather's disastrous year. She'd probably not been as sympathetic as she should have been, and she vowed to make it up to her granddaughter.

Christmas in The Meadows seemed almost like going back in time. They sat round the table in paper hats, telling jokes, while Bernard carved the turkey.

"You're not vegetarian any more, then, Heather?" chided her grandmother.

"No, and Mum's got over her phobia about poultry," responded Heather.

"That happened ages ago," retorted Katie. "I just didn't like eating the animals I had been caring for. That's natural, isn't it?"

"Good job you don't have cows and sheep and pigs then, isn't it?" said Robbie.

"You don't mind eating sheep, do you, Robbie?" asked Rose.

"No. That's what they're bred for. We look after them well. They have a happy life."

"Well no-one can turn their noses up at Christmas pudding or mince pies," said Katie. "Clear a space for the cream and sauce, please. There's too much cracker rubbish on the table."

Emboldened by drink, Bernard attempted to tell Katie what he and Zak had been planning. "When I went to see Zak in his hotel I met all the other disabled people with their helpers and they told me about the holidays they went on during the year. They have hotels all over the country that they visit and they go to stately homes and gardens, and sometimes to shows in the evenings. I told them I would like to volunteer. What do you think, Katie?"

"Would you have the same people every time?"

"I'm not sure. I didn't want to do anything until I'd asked you."

"I think you'd like it. You liked helping the people at

the horticultural college, didn't you?"

"It would mean I went away without you."

"That's not such a bad thing, as long as it's not too often. I was planning some changes, too. I want to let one of the bedrooms."

"Like Rose used to?"

"Yes, B and B. It's a pity the rooms are upstairs or we could have some of the people you want to help."

"Zak said it would be a good idea for me to learn sign language."

"For deaf people?"

"Yes. I'd like to do that."

"So would I. Perhaps we could both learn – then we would have a special service to offer. That's a wonderful idea, Ned."

He loved seeing her look so happy. It made Christmas the best he could ever remember.

They had a quiet New Year. Only Heather went out for the evening and she was back by one o'clock.

Rose hadn't seen the New Year in. She was staying with them as Katie had decided to let Pat's flat. "You never know – we might want to downsize one day," she'd told her mother. "I didn't want to let it go."

Rose was proud of her daughter. In spite of all her anxieties she had turned out to be wise and loving. She couldn't have asked for more.

She was looking forward to getting back to her own home. It felt as if she'd done the right thing now that Robbie was going to join her in Wales. Maybe it was fate that had sent her back to her grandmother's homeland.

Heather wasn't sure about her new environment.

The city wasn't the same as the one she was used to. It seemed more serious, less vibrant, with an even greater contrast of ancient and modern. Everyone seemed busy- trying so hard to compete, and yet occasionally she felt like a stranger in her own land.

I'll get used to it, she e-mailed Emma. *But I didn't realise how different the Midlands would be.*

The work is amazing. There is such a variety of problems, all types, all ages.

My lodgings are a bit dour, but the landlady is very kind. She looks a bit like Auntie Pat – big and bosomy, only her hair is dyed. Pat's was naturally red.

A new batch of servicemen came in today. The nurses say they react to being injured in so many different ways. Some are silent, some are angry and some make jokes. I'm seeing one tomorrow to help him get used to his prosthetic leg. I hope he's not one of the angry ones.

Love, H.

The injured soldier did not appear to be one of the angry ones. He was someone Heather knew. The injured soldier was Ryan.

He did not seem to recognise Heather at first, as she inspected him, got him to move his good leg and then strapped on his artificial one.

His face was grim – as if he was not going to let on, even if it did hurt him.

"Adjust your weight," she advised. "You're putting it all on the good leg."

"I'll not play rugby again, will I?" he muttered.

"Probably not – but people have run marathons with legs like these."

"You sound like someone I used to know – but she was

more southern."

"No, I'm not," she responded. "It's just that I trained up north."

"Heather? Is it you?"

"Yes, of course, silly. I'd say it was great to see you but it wouldn't sound right under the circumstances."

"Are you going to be my physio?"

"Yes, until you get out of here."

"Wow. What a turn up for the books."

"You'll have to do what I say, mind."

"Yes, ma-am. Just wait till I tell Mum and Dad."

"Do they know you're here?"

"Yes, someone from the regiment went and told them."

"How did you get injured?"

"A roadside I.E.D. Like all the others." He sounded bitter. "Nothing heroic, I'm afraid."

She wanted to say, 'I think you're heroic, just being there.' But it would have sounded unprofessional. She had to stay cool and not treat him any differently from her other patients.

He was different, though. In spite of the fact that she knew he didn't think of her that way she felt her old affection returning.

When she was with him she wanted to prolong the session, discover more about what he'd been doing in the intervening years.

When he was downhearted it made her miserable too, and doubly determined to help him recover and adjust.

He was not an easy patient. In fact, patient was not a word that could be applied to him. He railed and chafed at the restrictions his situation put him in.

One day when she went to take him through his exercises he was sullen and unresponsive. "Why is everyone trying to get me to walk?" he said. "Did you see those people in wheelchairs on TV? They were playing the most exciting game of basketball I have ever seen. I could do that, instead of staggering around like a bull elephant."

"What makes you think bull elephants stagger?"

"You know what I mean. I feel so clumsy. I suppose you're still dreadfully sporty?"

"No, actually. I had an accident over hurdles and couldn't race any more. Didn't your Mum tell you?"

"No. Not all her letters and parcels got through. How come you chose this job?"

"That was it, really. When I broke my leg the physio was so good I was impressed. I wanted to do that. I did a bit of swimming at Uni, but that was all."

She didn't want to think of what else she did while she was there.

She was glad Lisa hadn't told him all about her. He wouldn't know how she'd been jilted. He wouldn't know about Neal.

Thinking of Neal made her cautious. She feared her time with him had made her less likely to find another man who would take her on. Would they always be jealous of her first serious relationship? It had certainly made her think twice about trusting another man enough to get married.

Ryan was ready to go home. He could walk so well on his artificial leg that, to the casual eye, there looked to be nothing wrong with him.

"I have to decide whether I want to stay in the army," he told her.

"Would they really have you back?"

"I've been told so – but I'm not sure I want to stay. I'd rather do something different, like you did. If I could treat it as an opportunity instead of a disaster I'd feel better."

"I wish I could help."

"You've helped already. When I've decided I'll let you know. Perhaps you could come over for a holiday, like you did before."

"With the family, you mean?"

"No, stupid – by yourself."

"Don't be so cheeky. I'll think about it. Now, I've got other patients to see."

"Thanks again, Heather." He gave her a quick peck on the cheek and then left.

Heather's face burned. She wondered why he didn't realise that being close to him was keeping her alive. The time she spent away from him seemed to pass like an old black and white movie as against the vivid colours she experienced in his presence.

He'd sort of invited her to his home, hadn't he? It was when he was in one of his nice moods. When he was feeling down he had a fierce temper and would curse and call her names. She would miss him, but she had work to do and people who needed her just as much as he had.

It was two months before she heard from Ryan again. She'd begun to think she'd seen the last of Ryan Walsh. Once again her dreams had been shattered.

She had hoped he was missing her as much as she missed him but discovered that he'd sent a letter to the hospital addressed to *Heather Longman*. He hadn't even noticed that she was now Heather Long! When it reached her she opened it fearfully, not daring to hope that he still wanted to see her.

Dear Heather, he wrote. *I have decided to train as a teacher. Apparently there aren't enough male teachers in schools and although I don't have a degree my qualifications will get me on the course. Perhaps there are special rules for crippled soldiers who specialise in Maths.*

I start in September. Can you come for a holiday before then? Mum and Dad would love to see you. Yours, Ryan.

Can I? thought Heather. What have I been waiting for all these weeks?

She couldn't imagine Ryan as a teacher. Why hadn't she told him her phone number or her e-mail? What if his letter had gone astray, just because she'd changed her name?

She read it again. There was the address in the top right hand corner, but no phone number.

She'd have to reply. She'd go to see him before she went south. How long would he expect her to stay? She needed to talk to her mother.

18

The phone rang in The Meadows and Katie picked it up.

"Mum, can you do something for me?" asked Heather.

"Of course, love. It's great to hear from you. How's it all going?"

"The job? Fine. It's just that I've had someone we know as a patient."

"Who?"

"Ryan Walsh. He's not here now. He's gone home. He lost a leg in the war."

"Oh, dear – poor Lisa. She'll be devastated."

"It's not all bad news. He's walking again and he says he's going to be a teacher, but that's not why I rang. They've asked me to go and see them. Ryan sent a letter but no phone number and no e-mail. I know Lisa's on e-mail. Can you ask her when in July would be convenient and how long they mean me to stay? I'm too embarrassed to ask him."

"Does he know about Neal?"

"No. He's not asked. He doesn't think of me in that way, mum. I'm just a friend."

"Men. How do you feel about him?"

"I like him a lot but I'm not getting my hopes up. He could meet someone he really fancies in the next year."

Katie sighed. She'd always hoped that Heather and Ryan would end up together, but that sort of thing only happened in films. The poor man. She couldn't imagine how he must have suffered. "OK. I'll sound out Lisa. She didn't tell me he was back. She must have been waiting for good news."

Heather couldn't remember ever being so nervous. She could hardly breathe for wanting to see Ryan again. She'd got a new satnav, had programmed in his address and was driving across the country to see him.

A whole week! Lisa had said she could stay for a whole week, and longer if she wished, but she'd promised to go home for a few days afterwards.

Her mother had given Lisa Heather's e-mail address and Lisa had contacted her straight away.

Ryan says you have been a great help to him.

You will have to squash into the little box room but we'd love to have you stay with us.

Ryan's a bit moody – but I expect you're used to that. Thank goodness he's not going back. Love, Lisa.

Heather pulled up outside Lisa's house and clambered out of the driving seat.

She was stiff and tired, but the sight of Ryan coming to meet her made her forget all her aches and pains.

"Hi, Heather," he grinned, and walked past her to the boot. "Want a hand?"

Lisa came running out and hugged her tightly. "Come on in. Ryan will see to your luggage. Did you have a good journey? What about the traffic?"

"I'm fine. I'll just get my bag and jacket." She kept her head down to hide her blushes while she handed Ryan the car keys.

Ryan's strong, muscular arms were evident in his

tight T-shirt. If she hadn't known better she would have considered him to be in peak fitness. She began to think this holiday had been a mistake. It was making her want him even more than when she was treating him.

Lisa and John asked about her course and her new job and she tried to give them an idea of what was entailed.

"Your mother seems to have found her vocation at last," said Lisa.

"You know they're letting out Robbie's old room?" said Heather. "They have bookings for people from next month."

"And Robbie? He's happy?"

"Oh yes. He's in Wales with his beloved sheep."

"Your Nan must like that."

"Yes, everyone's settled except me." She could have bitten off her tongue as soon as she'd spoken. How could she have let herself sound so desperate? "Still, I'm going to look for a flat," she added. "I can't stay in lodgings all my life."

"Would you like to go swimming tomorrow?" asked Ryan.

"That would be great." She turned to him, grateful that the conversation had taken a new direction.

"I didn't go when I got back. I didn't fancy everyone staring at me but it will be OK with you there."

"Wimp!" she teased and watched his face light up.

She'd noticed how people who witnessed his disability treated him differently.

To her he was the same Ryan he had always been, someone she could relax and laugh with. She had no concerns that he would feel pitied by her. They'd spent enough time together in the weeks of his treatment to resume their previous friendship.

She had a restless night.

Thank goodness she took her swimming costume with her wherever she went. She'd seen Ryan splashing about in the hydrotherapy pool but she didn't know how well he could swim with only one leg. She'd have to be diplomatic and not try to race him.

"Can you manage your leg?" she asked as they bought their tickets.

"Yes, easy. I'll come out with it and leave it on the side – give everyone a laugh."

"There shouldn't be too many people in this early."

"That's why I said 8am. See you inside."

There were only a few people in the water when she reached the pool.

She watched while Ryan removed his leg, and then slid across to the steps and lowered himself into the water, holding onto the rail.

"Thanks," he said.

"What for?"

"For not rushing up to help me."

"I've got to have learnt something over the last few months."

"Right. How's your swimming?"

"Better than yours, as usual," and she set off down the pool.

She was surprised when she reached the deep end and he was still with her.

He shook the water out of his eyes and looked challengingly at her.

"Not bad," he said.

"Did you use the hospital pool when I wasn't around?"

"Well, you know yourself – if it's the only sport you can do, you do more of it."

"Is it the only sport you can do?"

He looked at her, then, as if she had struck a chord, staring as if he was seeing her for the first time. She could almost hear the cogs turning in his brain.

Had she meant to sound so suggestive? It certainly caused a reaction.

Still treading water, he reached out towards her and lost his balance, tipping sideways into the pool.

Had he been going to kiss her? It felt as if he might have – but the moment had passed and he was showing off, swimming underwater and between her legs.

She struck out and sped into racing mode, weaving between the other swimmers as she powered from end to end of the pool.

"I think that's enough," said Ryan when she paused for breath. "It's getting a bit crowded now."

She climbed out and made sure he was behind her and went for her shower.   Once dressed, she looked for the café area and sat by the window.

Suddenly she was overwhelmed by a feeling of sadness. It was too much like déjà vu. This was how her romance with Neal had started, and look where that had ended? She couldn't stay. She had to get out.

She looked round wildly for Ryan. He wasn't there yet. She didn't want to wait for him. She didn't want to be there any more. She didn't want to get hurt again.

She ran through the glass swing doors and stood, shaking, in the car park.

Why couldn't she control her feelings?

Why did she always have to fall for the most unsuitable men?

"Heather? Heather?" Ryan was calling her.

He was standing in the doorway of the swimming pool, looking concerned.

"What's up? Don't you want a drink? Are you OK?"

She turned back towards him, unable to stop the tears that were running down her face. "I'm sorry, Ryan. It's just brought back bad memories."

He came towards her and put his arms round her. She shook as she rested her head against his.

"Come back inside," he said. "Come and tell me all about it."

She did, then. She told him how she had met Neal, how she'd fallen in love with him and their plans to get married. She told him about the letter and the holiday in Mauritius. He laughed, then, and she was forced to smile. She told him she hadn't heard from Neal since he went to America.

She told him more than she'd ever told anyone before, and when she finished she felt drained and empty.

"What a complete bastard," he said at last. "You've been through even more than I have."

"That's not true," she argued. "But we've won through, haven't we?"

"I like that," replied Ryan.

"What?"

"The way you say 'We'. It makes us sound like a team."

He was absent-mindedly stroking her hair and, almost as if in a trance, bent to kiss it.

She looked round at him, at the face of the man she had almost always loved, and knew that this was the moment she had been waiting for all her life.

His mouth came down on hers in a gentle, lingering

kiss. He held her head between his hands and let his eyes roam across her features.

"You do know what you're taking on, don't you?" he asked.

"I didn't say I was taking on anything," she responded, knowing the delight on her face was giving her away.

He kissed her again, then, "Say you love me," he challenged.

"Of course I love you."

"Say you'll marry me."

"One day I'll marry you," and they collapsed in a huddle of laughter.

"Come on," he said, "Let's go and tell everybody. I've not felt like this in years."

"I've never felt like this," she said, grabbing his arm. "I never, ever want to let go of you again."